THE MONKS OF THELEMA: A NOVEL, IN THREE VOLUMES, VOL. III

Published @ 2017 Trieste Publishing Pty Ltd

ISBN 9780649651429

The Monks of Thelema: A Novel, in Three Volumes, Vol. III by Walter Besant & James Rice

Edited by Trieste Publishing Pty Ltd.
Cover @ 2017

www.triestepublishing.com

WALTER BESANT & JAMES RICE

THE MONKS OF THELEMA: A NOVEL, IN THREE VOLUMES, VOL. III

 Trieste

THE

MONKS OF THELEMA.

A Novel.

BY

WALTER BESANT AND JAMES RICE,

AUTHORS OF

"READY-MONEY MORTIBOY," "THE GOLDEN BUTTERFLY," "BY
CELIA'S ARBOUR," "THIS SON OF VULCAN," "MY LITTLE
GIRL," "THE CASE OF MR. LUCRAFT," "WITH HARP
AND CROWN," "WHEN THE SHIP COMES
HOME," ETC., ETC.

IN THREE VOLUMES.
VOL. III.

London:
CHATTO AND WINDUS, PICCADILLY.
1878.

THE MONKS OF THELEMA.

CHAPTER I.

" Or I am mad, or else this is a dream."

MRS. BOSTOCK continued to take the same gloomy view of Alma's wonderful fortune. Instead of rejoicing with her husband, and holding up her head as he did, she went about downcast and murmuring, instead of thanking Heaven. She said it was unnatural; she laughed to scorn her daughter's earnest efforts to make herself a lady ; she even went so far as to declare that it was a flying in the face of Providence.

There is only one manner of meeting with opposition possible to men whose powers of utterance are not equal to their powers of indignation. Everybody knows that method :

most women have experienced its force, and can testify to the remarkable lack of results which follow its exhibition. What one "damn," in fact, cannot effect, fifty cannot. Yet a certain artistic pride in rising to the occasion carries on the swearer. But even after the greatest provocation, followed by the most extraordinary efforts, you always feel, as a merchant skipper once complained to me with tears in his eyes, after swearing till the topmasts trembled, that you have hardly done justice to the subject. The Bailiff did his best, poor man ; and yet his wife remained obdurate.

No one sympathised with her, except, perhaps, Miranda, to whom she poured out her soul.

"How should the girl be fit," asked her mother, "to be a gentleman's wife ? It isn't from her father that she'd learn the soft ways that Master Alan has been used to, that's quite certain. Then he'll turn round some day and blame me for it—me, his mother's own maid, as held him in my arms before he was a day old !"

"But Alma looks soft and gentle," said

Miranda; "and I am quite sure that Alan would never impute any blame to you."

Mrs. Bostock spread out her hands and nodded her head.

"Soft and gentle!" she echoed. "Miss Miranda, a cat is soft and gentle; but a cat has got a temper. Only a cat has manners; which," she added, after a pause, "my daughter hasn't got."

"Bostock," she went on, "thinks it will be a fine thing for him. So it will, no doubt. Alma thinks it will be a fine thing to sham grand lady. Well, until she tires of it, no doubt it will be. Instead of learning her gratitude and duty to her husband—instead of trying to see how she can prevent being a shame and disgrace to him—goes into the village and flaunts round, trying to make that blacksmith's girl burst with spite, while her father goes to Athelston market, and makes believe he's equal to the biggest farmer in the place."

This was a gloomy, but a true picture.

"And no taste in dress," the ex-lady's-maid went on. "Anything that's got a colour in it: here a bit of red, and there a bit of

yellow. It makes me ashamed, I declare,
Miss Miranda, just to see you in that lovely
pearl-grey, so cool and sweet this hot morning, is a rest for weary eyes. There! you
always had, next to my lady, the true eye for
colour. That is born with a woman."

Then Miranda took the step which she had
been meditating since the first news of the
engagement. It was not a thing which gave
her any pleasure; quite the contrary. It
gave her a great deal of pain; it was a step
which would keep before her eyes a subject
on which she was compelled to think—Alan's
engagement and his *fiancée!* In fact, she
asked Mrs. Bostock to send Alma to Dalmeny
Hall, to stay with herself until the wedding.

Mrs. Bostock hesitated.

"Would Mrs. Dalmeny like it?"

" My mother is almost entirely confined to
her own room. Alma will see little or nothing
of her."

" And the ladies of Weyland Court?"

" Alma will probably see none of them,"
said Miranda, smiling. "We shall not make
her a Sister of our Monastery."

" It's more than kind of you, Miss Miranda,

and I know it is all for Mr. Alan's sake.
The banns are to be put up next Sunday,
and her things to be got ready and all. But
I can manage better without her, and up here
with you she will be out of mischief, and
learning nothing but what's good."

"Out of mischief, at least," said Miranda.

" Unless you're a lady, and can make your
daughter a lady," said Mrs. Bostock, " it's a
dreadful difficult thing to bring up a girl.
Full of deceit they are, and cunning as no
one would believe. Look as innocent, too, if
you trust their looks, which I don't, nor
wouldn't let one of them go out o' sight for
five minutes. Even now, while I'm here, I
shouldn't wonder if Alma isn't carrying on
with—— But she shan't say I made mischief," concluded the good woman, as if her
whole discourse had tended to the praise and
honour of her daughter.

Alma was not " carrying on" with any one.
She was harmlessly employed before the
biggest looking-glass in the house, practising
the art of walking as she had seen Miss Nelly
walk, with her long skirts gathered up in the
left hand, and a parasol in the right. She

worked very hard at this imitation, and really succeeded in producing a fair caricature.

It must be acknowledged that, so far, Alma's only gratification in her engagement was this kind of exercise. Whatever else would happen to her, whatever "rows"—this young lady confidently expected rows—with her husband, whatever defiance or disobedience she would have to exhibit, one thing was quite certain, that she should be a lady. She would have her servants and her carriage ; she would have as many dresses, and as fine, as she wished.

Her only gratification—worse than that, her only consolation ! The prospect of actual marriage with that grave and solemn man, full of books and things beyond all comprehension, was becoming daily more repugnant. She was not a girl of strong will ; she was afraid of her father, of Mr. Dunlop, and of Harry. She was afraid of all three, and she could not bear to think of the consequences which might follow whatever line she adopted. As for the grandeur of the thing, the poor girl was already *désillusionnée.* Grandeur with perpetual company manners was not, she felt, worth the fuss people made about it. All very well to flaunt in the face of Black Bess, and the like of her ; but a *gêne* when one is alone, or surrounded by those very wearying companions, stiff manners and incomprehensible talk.

Three weeks before the wedding. A good deal may be done in three weeks, did one only know the right thing to do. A clear run of three weeks, which she had hoped to use for some good purpose, to be devised by Harry, at home. And now she was to give up this precious interval of liberty, and spend it in learning company manners at Dalmeny Hall —company manners all day long, and no relaxation.

And she had begun, in her foolish and irrational jealousy, to hate Miss Dalmeny, whom, in former days, she had only envied. The young lady represented all that her betrothed regarded as perfect in womanhood. Can a girl be expected to fall in love with some one else's ideal—her engaged lover's ideal—of what she herself might be ? It is not in human nature.

She dared not yet show her animosity.

Once married, she thought, Miss Dalmeny
should see of what a spirit she could be.
Only, when Alan talked of Miranda, she set
her lips together and was silent; and when
Miranda came to see her, she hung her pretty
head and became sulky.

Miranda saw the feeling, and partly guessed
its cause.

It was impossible for Alma to refuse an invitation at which Alan was rejoiced beyond
measure, and her father gratified, because it
seemed, to his amazing conceit, as if the
whole world was ready to acknowledge the
fitness of the match.

" My little gell," he said, rubbing his great
red hands together, and assuming an expression of gratified vanity, which made Alma
long to spring to her feet and box his ears for
him—it is understood that young ladies with
such fathers as Stephen Bostock accept the
Fifth Commandment with a breadth of view
which allows large deductions—" my little
gell is to be received at Dalmeny Hall. She
is not to walk there, if you please, nor is she
to go in by the back way——"

" Like her mother," interposed Mrs. Bostock.

" She will be drove there by Miss Miranda
herself," resumed her husband. " She will
be bowed down before and scraped unto by
the footmen, and the butler, and the coach-
man, and the lady's-maid. She will be made
a lady before Mr. Alan makes her a lady."

" I wish being a lady wasn't all company
manners," sighed Alma.

" Think of the grandeur !" said her father.
" Think of setting alone on your own sofy at
Weyland Court—because that's all nonsense
what Mr. Alan talks—and receiving your
father when he calls to see you. You will be
grateful then to your father for being such
a father, as it does a gell credit to take
after."

Miranda drove her pony-carriage to the
farm to take her. She saw that the girl was
unwilling to come, and she guessed, from the
red spot in her cheeks, and her lowering
look, that there had been some difference of
opinion between her and her mother. In
fact, there had been a row royal, the details
of which present nothing remarkable. The
contention of Mrs. Bostock, had the matter
been calmly argued, was that her daughter's

disinclination to spend the three weeks
before her wedding at Dalmeny Hall was
another proof of her unfitness to rise to the
greatness which was thrust upon her. Nothing but a natural love for low life and
conversation, such as her father's, could
account for her wish to refuse the invitation.
Alma would have pleaded, had not temper
got the better of reason, that he might have
allowed her to enjoy in her own way the last
three weeks of her liberty.

The controversy, warmly maintained on
either side, was raging at its height when
Miss Dalmeny's ponies were seen coming up
the road from the village. Both disputants
instantly became silent.

Very little was said when Alma left her
home, and scant was the leave-taking she
bestowed upon her parent. But her heart
sank when the thought came upon her that
she was leaving the old life altogether, never
to come back to it, and that for the future it
would be always company manners.

Mrs. Bostock watched the carriage drive
away. She, too, felt a heart-sinking. Her
daughter was gone.

" A son is a son till he marries a wife,
  A daughter's a daughter all her life."

It was not so in her case. She knew that,
lady or not, there would be a space between
her and Alma more widening as she acquired
new ideas, and began to understand how a
lady thinks of things. And spite of her
temper, her craft, and her subtlety, the good
woman was fond of her daughter. Now
Alma was gone, she would be left alone with
her Stephen, and he with the thirst for
brandy-and-water growing upon him. What
difference did a little quarrel, however fierce,
make for mother or daughter ?

Alma preserved her silence and sulkiness
during their short drive to Dalmeny Hall.
It made her worse to observe that Black Bess
was not in the village to watch her driving in
state with Miss Dalmeny.

Miranda took her to her own room, a pretty
little room, furnished with luxury to which
the Bailiff's daughter was wholly unaccus-
tomed. The aspect of the dainty white cur-
tains, the pretty French bed, the sofa, the
toilet-table, the great glass, took away her
breath, but it did not take away her sulki-

ness.   She reflected that all these pretty
things meant company manners—why, oh !
why, cannot people have nice things, and
yet live anyhow ?—and she hardened her
heart.

"This is your room, Alma," said Miranda.   "I hope you will be happy with
us."

Alma sat on the bed, and began to pull off
her gloves, pulling at them with jerks.

"You don't really want me," she said
slowly, glancing furtively at her hostess, for
she was dreadfully afraid.   "You don't really
want me here at all.   You only want to
teach me manners.   You want to improve
me before I am married, that's all."

It was quite true, but not a thing which
need be said openly.

"Come, Alma," said Miranda kindly ;
"you are going to marry Alan.   Is not that
reason enough for our being friends ?"

But Alma went on pouting and grumbling.

"That's all very well, and if I hadn't been
going to marry Mr. Dunlop, of course you
wouldn't have noticed me no more than the
dirt beneath your feet.   I know that.   But

it's all nonsense wanting to be friends. You think you can teach me how to behave so as he shan't be ashamed of me. Very well, then. I always thought, till I was engaged to a gentleman, that I knew as well as anybody. But I know now that I don't. Mr. Dunlop, he's always saying that there's nobody like you in all the world." Here Miranda blushed violently. "Why didn't he ask you to marry him, then, instead of me? I'm to imitate you if I can, he says. Then mother keeps nagging—says I'm not fit to sit at table with gentlefolks. It isn't my fault. Why did she not teach me? She ought, because she knows, though father doesn't."

"Manners," said Miranda, "are chiefly a matter of good feeling."

Here she was quite wrong. In my limited pilgrimage, I have met abundant examples of men possessing excellent hearts and the kindest dispositions, who seemed to regard a plate as a trough. I am not at present thinking of the *commis voyageurs* whom you meet at French country town *tables d'hôte*, because their hearts are not commonly considered to be in the most desirable place.

Then Miranda took Alma's red hand—it was shapely and small—in her own white fingers, and pressed it kindly.

"Come, my dear, we will improve each other."

They had luncheon together, and alone. In the afternoon they sat in Miranda's cool morning-room, which looked upon the shady garden, and while the bees droned heavily outside among the flowers, and the light breeze rustled among the leaves, and the heavy scent of summer floated through the open windows, Miranda told the girl something—she did not trust herself to tell her all —of Alan's life.

"And so you see, my dear, his whole life, from the very first, as soon as he understood that he was born to wealth, has been an endeavour to find out how best to use that wealth, not for any personal advantage or glory, but for the good of others. And while other rich men have contented themselves with giving money, speaking on platforms, and leaving secretaries to do the work, he put his theories into practice, and has always worked himself instead of paying others to work. He has thought out the kind of life which he believes will be of the greatest benefit, and he has lived that life. I think, Alma, that there is no man living who has so much courage and such strength of will as Alan."

" Yes," said Alma thoughtfully. " Father always did say that he was more cracked than any man he'd ever come across. And I suppose he is."

This was not quite Miranda's position, but she let it pass.

" To live among the people as one of themselves, to live as they live, to eat among them, sleep among them, and to show them how the higher life is possible even for the poorest, surely, Alma, that is a very noble thing to do."

Alma looked as if she should again like to quote her father, but would refrain. Those who dwell habitually among the lower sorts acquire an insight into the baser side of human nature which, perhaps, compensates for the accompanying incredulity as to noble or disinterested actions.

Alma did not quote Mr. Bostock, but she

laughed, being on this subject as incredulous as Sarai.

"After all, what good has he done the villagers with his notions?" she asked.

"Who can tell?" replied Miranda. "You cannot sow the seed altogether in vain. Some good he must have done."

"He hasn't, then," said Alma triumphantly. "Not one bit of good. If I wasn't afraid of him, I'd tell him so myself. You might, because you are not going to marry him, and have no call to be afraid."

Miranda shuddered. Was this girl chosen on purpose to carry on Alan's schemes, going to begin by openly deriding them?

Alma lay back in her easy-chair—in spite of company manners, the chair was delicious —and went on with her criticism of Alan's doings.

"Stuff and rubbish it all is, and stuff and rubbish I've called it all along. There was the Village Parliament. When the beer stopped, that stopped. Not one single discussion was held there. Only the usual talk about pigs and beer—same as in the Spotted Lion. Then there was the shop, where everybody was to have little books, and put down what they bought, and have a profit in it at the end of the year. As if the people would take that trouble! And there was no credit, until the boys gave credit, contrary to orders. And then there was the Good Liquor Bar, where the beer was to be sold cheap, and the best. Why they used to water the beer, those two boys, and unless they'd given credit, too, no one would have ever had a glass there. And you know how both the boys have run away with all the money, and Mr. Dunlop's found out that they kept a double set of books."

"Yes," said Miranda: "It is such a pity that dishonesty must be taken into account in every plan."

"All the village knew about it—at least, all the women. Then the men on father's farm got three shillings a week extra. That makes all the other men jealous. For do you think that the men took the money home to their wives? Not they, nor wouldn't if it had been thirty shillings. Spent it all, every drop, in beer."

She almost rose to the level of righteous
indignation as she made these revelations.

" And the Library ! That makes a nice
place for Prudence Driver. She—and a
nasty little cat she is—tried to get Mr. Dunlop to listen to her tales and gossip. Well,
we shall see before long."

Miranda began to feel very uncomfortable
indeed. The young lady was revealing the
seamy side to her character.

" And the Baths ! As if those beer-drink-
ing louts ever wanted to wash. It's too
ridiculous. Well, I hope Mr. Dunlop's had
enough of his foolishness now. I'm afraid to
tell him. But I hope you will, Miss Dalmeny."

" We will grant," said Miranda, with a
feeling of hopelessness, because the girl could
not even feel respect for Alan's self-sacrifice—
" we will grant that some of the experiments
have not been successful. You, however,
Alma, are his last experiment. It depends
upon yourself whether you will be successful."

" Oh ! yes," sighed the girl wearily. " He's
always talking, but I can't understand, and

sometimes I listen and sometimes I don't. Said once he wanted to marry me in order to enter more fully into their minds. Their minds, indeed! As if that would help him. I always thought men married girls because they loved them—and never a word, not one single syllable about love. How would you like it, Miss Dalmeny ?"

Miranda could not help it. The feeling was unworthy, but her heavy heart did lift a little at the thought that Alan had made no pretence of love to this girl.

" Then he lends me books. Books about all sorts of things. Books so stupid, that you would think no one would ever be found to read them."

" But you do read them ?"

" Oh! I pretend, you know. I tried to, first of all, but it was no use; and then, because I saw he liked it, I took to pretending." This she confessed with the perfect confidence that among persons of her own sex such little deceptions are laudable when found expedient.

And so the truth was at last ascertained by Miranda. The girl, in spite of all Alan's preachings, which had fallen upon unlistening ears, was wholly unprepared for the life designed for her, and perfectly ignorant of her suitor's designs.

What was to be done ?   She was afraid to tell Alan, and she shrank from telling Alma. Then she sent a note to Desdemona, asking her to come to her help.   Desdemona came to dinner, and after dinner—which Alma thought a most tedious and absurdly ceremonious affair—Miranda played and sang a little, while Desdemona talked to Alma.

She talked artfully, this craftiest of comedians.   She congratulated Alma on her success of the Golden Apple, which she insinuated was the means by which her splendid subsequent success had been brought about. And when Alma, who found in her a person much more sympathetic than Miss Dalmeny, at once plunged into her private grievances at being deprived of the usual accompaniments of courting, Desdemona murmured in tones of real feeling, " Dear ! dear me ! how very sad ! and how very strange !"

And then she added, as if the thing made Alan's coldness conspicuously disgraceful :

" And when, too, he is going to make you sacrifice yourself in that dreadful way !"

" What dreadful way ?" asked Alma.

" Why, my dear child, after your marriage."

" After my marriage. What do you mean, Mrs. Fanshawe ?"

" Why, my dear, what do you think you will do when you are married ?"

Miranda heard the question, and went on playing softly.

" Why . . . live at Weyland Court, to be sure ; and have carriages and servants, and be a lady."

" But that is not at all what you will do," said Desdemona. " Has not Alan told you ?"

Alma's face grew white.

" You will never live at Weyland Court at all," said Desdemona, slowly and icily. " The Court will be let to other people. You will have no carriages and no servants : you will live in the village among the people : you will work as you do now : you will lead the same homely life that you have always led, only simpler : yet it will be necessary, for your husband's sake, that you make yourself a lady.

It will be your lifelong business to show the
villagers how a cottage woman may be a
lady."

Alma gasped.

" Is this the meaning of all his talks that I
never listened to ?"   She sprang to her feet
and clasped her hands.   " Oh ! I am cheated
—I am cheated !   And why did he pick me
out for such foolery ?"

" Because," said Miranda, leaving the piano
and looking her sternly in the face, " because
Alan thinks that he has found a woman who
will enter into his noble plans, and help him
to carry them out.   Because he trusts entirely
in your loyalty and truth, Alma.   And because
he thinks that you, too, desire a life which
shall be one of self-sacrifice, and yet most
beautiful and holy for him and for you."

But Alma broke out into passionate crying
and sobbing.   She asked if this was to be the
end of her fine engagement, that everybody
was to laugh at her, that she was to be worse
off than Black Bess, and her wedding only
land her among the wash-tubs of the rustics.
She was a practical young lady, and life in a
cottage without a servant suggested wash-

tubs as the prominent feature. And then, in an uncontrollable rage, she sprang to her feet, and cried :

" I might have had Harry Cardew, and he's a man and not a milksop."

And then she sat down again in her chair, and sobbed again.

Presently she plucked up her spirits a little, left off crying, and stated calmly her intention of going to bed, to avoid being laughed at any more.

No opposition was made to this proposal, except a faintly deprecatory remark by Miranda, to the effect that they were very far from laughing at her.

When she was gone, the two ladies looked at each other.

" My dear Desdemona," said Miranda, " my heart is very heavy for poor Alan."

" He is not married yet," said Desdemona. Really, that was getting a formula of hers.

Miranda, presently, instead of going to her own room, sought Alma's. The poor girl had cried herself to sleep, and lay with her tear-stained cheek on her open hand—a pic-

ture for a painter. Alma in repose, Alma
asleep, Alma motionless, was like a possible
Greuze. You thought, as you looked at the
parted lips and the closed eyes, what the face
would be like when the lips were parted for
a smile, and the eyes were dancing with delight or languid with love. But when the lips
were parted for a smile, it was generally a
giggle or a feminine sneer—when the eyes
were dancing with delight, it was joy at
another's misfortunes ; and if they were ever
soft and languid with love, it was not when
they looked in the face of Alan Dunlop, but
in that of Gamekeeper Harry. For Alma
was all her fond mother painted her : a young
lady of unpolished manners and low views
of life.

Miranda set down her candle, and sat
awhile looking at the girl who had robbed her
of the one man she could ever love. It
seemed cruel. He would not and did not
pretend to love this village maiden : she
made no pretence of any sort of affection for
him. She didn't even regard him with respect.
She thought him cracked. She did not understand, even now, what he wanted her for ;

there was not the smallest possibility that she would ever rise to understanding him. She was no helpmeet for him, and he, with his enthusiasm and simple loyalty, was no fit husband for her. But Miranda could do nothing.

Presently, the light awakened Alma, who sat up, startled, and seeing Miranda, began to cry again, partly because she was rather ashamed of her recent outbreak.

"My poor child," said Miranda, taking her hand and sitting down beside her; "I am so sorry. I thought you knew the whole of Alan's designs."

"I di—didn't listen," she said. "It all seemed so stupid, and, oh! I did think I should be made a lady."

"So you will, Alma, if you choose to be a lady. No one could live with Alan Dunlop without becoming nobler and better. My dear, there is nothing to cry about. You will have the best husband in the world, and he will smooth your path for you. It will be your happy task to show the villagers the beauty of a modest life. Alma, you will be

envied in the long run, far more than if you
were going to Weyland Court to live in idle-
ness.   You will think of things in this way,
won't you ?"

"I'll try to," said Alma.   "But, oh! he's
cheated me."

Miranda stole away.   "He" was no doubt
Alan, and it was a bad omen of the future
when she prefaced her promised medita-
tions on the Higher Life with the observation that her guide and leader had cheated
her.

Next day, Gamekeeper Harry received, by
hand, two letters.   This greatly astonished
him, as he was not in the habit of maintaining
a correspondence with any one.   The first,
written in a fine Italian hand which was difficult for the honest fellow to read, was given
him by a footman in the Thelema livery.   It
was signed "Clairette Fanshawe"—I think
I have already alluded distantly to the fact that
Sister Desdemona's marriage having proved
a failure, she had long since resumed her
maiden name with the marriage prefix—and
asked him simply to call upon the writer at
the Abbey that same afternoon, if possible.

He accepted the appointment by word of mouth with the footman.

The other letter was brought by a boy—in fact, the son of an under-gardener. He drew it from the inside of his cap, and gave it to Harry with a show of great secrecy.

"Oh! Harry," the letter began. It was written in a hand which was legible, but yet not clerkly. "Oh! Harry—such a revelation as you little dream of! and what to do—with Mr. Dunlop on one side and Miss Miranda on another, both at me like printed books, and Mrs. Desdy Moner, as they call her, who was nothing but a painted actress and glories in it, with her scornful ways about my not going to Weyland Court after all. I don't know what to do nor where to turn. So if you can help me, and mean to, now's the time. And I'll try to be at the little gate at the end of the garden—that which Mr. Dunlop always uses, and it opens on the park— at nine o'clock; and do you be there, too, punctual. To think of living in the village alongside of Black Bess, and she to come out and laugh all day long, and me to go on slaving worse than at home.

" Your miserable true love,

" ALMA."

Said Gamekeeper Harry to Robert the boy: " You tell her, boy, that I've read the letter and I'll be there."

CHAPTER II.

"'Are you going to be a fool?' asked George.
"'Of course I am not going to be a fool,' answered the young woman."

TROLLOPE.

BEFORE six the next morning Alma awoke according to usual custom. It took her a few moments to remember everything, that she was in one of the rooms of Dalmeny Hall, the scene of last night, her tears and disappointment. But the knowledge came all too quickly, and she sprang from the bed and began to dress herself swiftly.

Then she sat down to the table, where the thoughtful Miranda had provided pens and paper, and dashed off the letter we know of already with the ease of a practised pen and the impetuosity of a war correspondent.

Then she recollected that it was only half
an hour's walk to the village of Weyland
across the park, that she could get there, see
her father at his breakfast, lay the whole
horrid truth before him, and be back again at
the Hall before Miss Dalmeny came down.
She slipped down the stairs as lightly as
Godiva ; the house was silent and shut up.
The great front doors were locked and barred,
and the shutters up, and the door which led
into the garden was closed in the same
manner.   She made her way into one of the
rooms — she did not know which — on the
ground-floor, and managed with some difficulty to open the shutters.   The window
looked out upon the garden, and on the lawn
was a boy whom she knew, an under-gardener's son, sweeping and tidying up.

" Robert !" she cried, in a loud whisper.

Robert looked up, and saw, to his amazement, Alma Bostock.

" Robert, I want to get out, and the doors
are locked.   Bring me a ladder, or the steps,
or something."

The window was about eight feet from the
ground.   Robert brought her his short gar-

deners' ladder, and the young lady, with much agility, proceeded to get out of the window and to descend. Seen from the outside, it looked like an elopement.

" Now, Robert," she said, " you go up the ladder and shut the window. They will think the shutters were left open by accident, and if anybody asks you about me, you didn't see me go out of the house, mind."

" I mind," said the boy, grinning.

" And, Robert," she went on, hesitating, " can I trust you, Robert ?"

He grinned again.

" I want you to take a letter for me, to Harry Cardew. You know where to find him ?"

" I know," said the boy.

" Then here is the letter. Let no one see you give it him. Hide it in the lining of your cap—so !—and I'll give you the very first shilling I get."

" I'll take it safe and quiet," said the boy stoutly.

She sped down the garden, out by the garden gate, and ran as fast as she could across the dewy grass of the park. Nobody

was there but the deer, who thought it a
shame that they should be disturbed so early
in the morning, and looked at her as indig-
nantly as the natural benignity of their eyes
enabled them, refusing entirely to get up and
scamper away, as they would do later on.

Fortunately, there was no necessity to go
through the village, so that she was seen by
no one : and she reached the farm before her
father—who in these days of fatness was
growing late in his habits—had left the house
on his early round.   And she was so early,
that it was yet an hour from their breakfast.

She rushed in, breathless and exhausted,
with eager eyes, as if something dreadful had
happened ; so much so, that her mother was
fain to sit down and gasp, and her father
stayed his hand which was grasping his hat.

" Alma !"

" Yes, father," she replied with short gasps.
" Yes, mother : well may you say ' Alma !'
Oh ! the things I've discovered.   Oh ! the
plots and the conspiracies !"

The Bailiff turned very pale.   Had anything happened then ?   Was the match, on
which, to him, everything depended, in

danger ? Had these plots anything to do with him ?

"We've been nicely fooled, all of us. Oh ! nicely fooled. And you, too, father," added Alma, "wise as you think yourself."

"Who's been a fooling of me ?" asked Mr. Bostock, proceeding, in general terms familiar to his daughter, to state the certain fate of the one who made a fool of Stephen Bostock.

"Mr. Dunlop, and Miss Dalmeny with him. They're them that have fooled us all," cried Alma, breathless. "What do you think he wants to marry me for ?"

"To make you his wife, I suppose," said her father. "That's what most men want, and a most uncommon stupid want it is."

"Ah !" his wife echoed, "for once you're right, Stephen."

"Then it isn't," said Alma ; "and you're just wrong. He doesn't want to make me his wife a bit ; that is, he won't make me a lady."

"Nobody ever thought he would, Alma," said her mother, staunch to her principles.

"He can't help it, Alma," said her father. "The wife of the Squire *must* be a lady : she's a lady by position. When a woman marries, she takes the rank of her husband. When I married you "—he nodded to his wife, formerly lady's-maid—" you took my position."

It was one of the minor results of the new allowance that the Bailiff had taken to consider himself a man of high, and even dignified, social position.

" That was fine promotion," said his wife. " Go in, Alma."

" You don't understand—neither of you understand. I thought I was going to be Mrs. Dunlop in proper style up at the Court and all. Well, it seems he's been explaining to me ever since we were engaged what he meant. It isn't that a bit. But I've been that stupid, as I wouldn't understand one word he said, and the more he said, the less I understood. It was Miss Miranda who told me the truth last night. Ah! father, you and your fine plans indeed!"

" What the devil is it, then ?"

" It's this. I'm not to go to the Court at all—I am never to go there. I'm to be kept hidden away down here in the village. I'm to live in a pigsty, like what Mr. Dunlop

has lived in for a year. We're to have no
servants—no nothing. I'm to do all the work
all day long, and listen to him talking all the
evening. Father, he'll drive me mad! What
with the work and the talk, I shall go
cracked!"

She shook her pretty head tragically, and
sat down on one of the wooden kitchen chairs
with a desperate sigh.

" But you will be married," said her father,
thinking of himself. " You'll be married to
the Squire. You can't well get over that.
Mr. Dunlop will be my son-in-law."

" And no fine dresses, and no pony-car-
riages, and nothing grand at all! And I'm
to make friends with all the women in the
village, and show them how they ought to
live ; and I shall be as poor as any of them,
because we shall live on five-and-twenty
shillings a week. Mother, I'd rather come
back home and work in the dairy again."

"So you shall," said her mother, " and
welcome. I always said it was unnatural."

" You keep your oar out of it," Mr. Bostock observed to his wife with firmness, " and
let me think this out a bit."

He sat in his arm-chair, his stick between his legs, and thought it out for ten minutes.

"I remember now," he murmured, "the Squire did talk about setting examples and that sort of stuff.   He's full of soft places, is the Squire."

Then he relapsed into hard thinking.

Meantime, the mother looked blankly at her daughter.   It was hard enough to realise that her lady's son could positively prefer her Alma to Miss Miranda.   It was still harder to understand why he wanted her to live with him in a cottage after the manner of the rustics, in order to set an example.   Did not Miss Miranda set an example to all the world of a beautiful young lady leading the most beautiful of lives ?   What else did he want ?

"And what," the girl went on with choking voice—"what will Black Bess say ?   And what will Prudence Driver say ?—the nasty, spiteful, little, twisted thing !   And what will all of them say ?"

"As for that," said Mrs. Bostock, "I suppose they will say just what they like.   You can't tie tongues.   It isn't that as I care about ; nor it isn't that as your father thinks about."

"No," said Alma, who had taken the bit between her teeth altogether since her engagement, and now permitted herself to criticise her parents with the greatest freedom. "All you care about is to stop the wedding if you can. You think your own daughter is a disgrace to Mr. Dunlop. In all the story-books I ever read yet, I never heard of a mother spiting her own daughter. Step-mothers a-plenty, but never a real mother. You ought to be ashamed of yourself, mother."

Mrs. Bostock began what would have proved too long a speech for insertion in these pages, but she was interrupted by her daughter, who now turned with vehemence upon her father.

"And as for you," she cried, with such force that the thinker, who was resting his chin on the stick, having closed his eyes for greater abstraction, sprang erect in his chair, and gazed at her with open mouth—"as for you, what you care about is to call Mr. Alan your son-in-law, and squeeze all you can out

of him.   I'm to marry the man for you to get
his money."

Mr. Bostock, recovering his self-possession,
remarked that, as a general rule, sauce is the
mother of sorrow, and cheek the parent of
repentance ; but that in this particular case
his daughter's provocations being such as they
were, he was prepared to overlook her breach
of the Fifth Commandment, of which, when
she fully understood a fond father's projects
and counsel, she would repent upon her
bended knees.   That is, he said words to
that effect in the Bostockian tongue.   After
which he relapsed into silence, and went on
considering the situation.

It seems extraordinary that not one of these
good people should before this have realised
the true position of things.   Alma, however,
heard the truth from Alan's lips once, and
once only, and then she was too confused to
understand.   Later on, when Alan repeated
in genial terms, again and again, his plan of
life, the girl was not listening.   Mrs. Bostock
had never heard the truth at all.   The Bailiff
understood only—we must remember that he
too, for private reasons, was confused on the

first hearing of the statement—that Alan was going to give up actual farm-work. And this being the case, there seemed really no reason at all why he should not go back and live in his own great house.

And now Alma's greatness was to be shorn of all but barren honour. And what for himself? Mr. Bostock went on meditating.

"What's the good of being the Squire's wife," asked Alma, " if I'm to be his kitchen drudge as well? Thank you for nothing. I'll stay at home, and let him marry Black Bess if he likes. I won't marry him at all."

Then Mr. Bostock, having arrived at a definite conclusion, slowly untwisted his right leg, which he had twined round the left calf, raised himself in his chair, and gazed steadfastly and in silence on his daughter.

Then he rose, took hat and stick, and spoke.

" You'll take a little walk with me, Alma," he said.

Mrs. Bostock saw that the parental advice would be such as she would not approve, but

it was no use for her to interfere, and she was
silent.

Outside the house her father thus addressed
Alma :

" The Squire is a-going to marry you, my
gell.   He will live, he says, down in the village, along with the farm-labourers, you and
him together.   Gar ! in a cottage where you
will do all the housework.   He's mad enough
to want that, and obstinate enough for anything.   But there's one thing he's forgotten."

"What's that, father ?"

"When he asked for you, I told him you
took after your father.   But I didn't tell him
that my gell had got a temper of her own,
like her father.   She is not one to be put
upon, nor is she one to be deprived of her
rights."

" But I'm so afraid of him."

" Ta, ta ! afraid of your husband, and you
a Bostock ?   You'll sort him once you get
the use of your tongue, free as you have been
accustomed to have it in your humble 'ome.
Lord ! I see it all reeling out straight before
me.   First the church, then the cottage ; that

may last a week or a fortnight, according as
you feel your way and get your freedom.
Then, one morning, you sit down and fold
your arms, and you says, ' Take me to Weyland Court,' you says ; ' that's the place where
I belong, and that's the place where I mean
to go. He begins to talk, you put on your
bonnet, and you walk up to Weyland Court,
willy-nilly, whether he comes or whether he
stays behind, and you sit down there, and
there you stay. You send for your old
father, and he will come and back you up.
Do you think he can drag you out of your
own house ? Not a bit of it."

" But he doesn't love me a bit, and he's
head over ears with Miss Dalmeny."

" Love ! stuff and rubbish ! Now look
here, Alma. Don't mix up foolishness.
You've got to marry him. I can't afford to
let the chance go. If you prefer the work'us,
say so, and go there—you and your mother.
Love ! what's love, if you've got your carriage and pair ? What's love when you can
walk up to the church a Sundays with the
folk scraping a both sides ? What's love
when you can have a new silk gownd every

day ? What's love with no more trouble about money ? Gar ! you and your love !"

Alma had nothing to say to this.

" And now, my gell," resumed her father, " you just go straight back to the Hall, and you'll get there before breakfast, and go on as meek as a kitten with them all ; and if they show their pride, remember that your time is coming. And your father's to give you away in the church, and to back you up when you do sit in your own house and laugh at 'em all. As for they lazy Monks, we'll soon send them about their business."

Thus dismissed, the girl walked slowly back to the Hall. What her father said was just. She might, by being bold at the right moment, assert herself, and reign at Weyland Court. On the other hand, she did not feel confidence in her own powers, and she was, besides, profoundly humiliated. She wanted revenge, and she did not comprehend, as her father saw, that her most efficacious revenge, as well as her wisest plan, would be to marry Alan first, and upset all his plans afterwards.

She got back before breakfast, and found

Miranda in the garden. She told her hostess that she had run across the Park to see her mother.

After breakfast, she sat in Miranda's room with one of Alan's selected books in her hand, and pretended to read.

As was this room, so, she supposed, were all the rooms of Weyland Court. It would be pleasant to sit in such rooms, to roam from one to the other, to feel herself the mistress. Pleasant, that is, if Mr. Dunlop was not there too. Pleasant, if you could slip into the garden and meet Harry Cardew. And here her heart fell low, because, as she reflected, after she was married, she would never, never see Harry any more.

In her way—her shallow way—Alma was certainly in love with this man. He had taken her fancy ; and to think of giving him up, and taking in his place the grave and solemn gentleman with the soft, cold manners, the deep and earnest eyes, whose every word fell upon her like a reproach ! Then her heart hardened, and Weyland Court, with all its glories, seemed a poor return for life spent with such a man.

Presently, looking up from her book, into whose pages she was gazing while she worked out these problems, she saw that she was alone. Miranda had left her. Alma tossed the book away, and began impatiently to wander round the room. First she looked at herself in the mirrors, of which there were two ; then she looked at the books and the pretty things on the tables ; and then she went to the window and began to yawn. Did ladies do nothing all day but sit over books ?

While she was still yawning, the door opened, and the lady they called Desdemona appeared. She was in walking-dress, having just come over from the Abbey, and as Alma looked at her, she felt as if she was at last looking into the face of a real friend.

Desdemona's face was capable of expressing every passion at will, but chiefly she excelled in conveying the emotion of sympathy. Her face this morning expressed sympathy in abundant measure. Sympathy beamed from the pose of her head—a little thrown back, because Alma was a little taller than herself, and a little thrown on one side—

from the softened eyes, from the parted lips, and from the two hands, which were held out to greet the village maid. I have never seen any actress who equalled Desdemona in the expression of pure, friendly, womanly sympathy.

"Oh! my dear," she began, taking both Alma's hands and squeezing them softly, "my dear, I *was* so sorry for you last night, so very sorry. How I felt for your sad position. And to think that he never told you! And we knew it all the time. What a pity! Oh! dear, dear! what a pity!"

"Perhaps he told me, but I was not listening."

"Such a pity! It seems so very hard upon you. What is the good of marrying a rich man if you have to be a poor woman?"

"Why, that's just what I told mother this morning," said Alma eagerly.

"Yes, and to think, oh! to think "—Desdemona's manner became sympathetic to the highest degree, and she almost wept with sympathy, and her voice trembled—"to think that you should *have* to listen to him, whatever he says, as soon as you are married !"

Alma groaned.

" And men—oh ! my dear, I know them well—are so fastidious.   You will have to do all the work of the house, make the beds, wash the linen, scrub the floors, scour the pots, cook the dinner, serve the breakfast and the tea, wash up the cups, and all ; and he will expect the manner—I mean the appearance—and dress of a lady with it all.   My poor dear ! no lady could do it.   It is not to be expected."

" Of course not," said Alma ; " but you are the first person to find it out.   Miss Dalmeny, I suppose, thinks it's as easy as easy."

" Miss Dalmeny does not know anything, my dear," said the perfidious Desdemona, with almost a gush of sympathy.   " And then, in addition to all that, you will have to go about among the labourers' wives and make friends of them.   That will be a very hard thing to do, for I am sure, my dear, such a pretty and well-mannered girl as yourself has never had much to do with that class of people."

" Indeed," said Alma. " I always despised the whole lot. Black Bess is no better than a labourer's daughter, and half a gipsy, too."

" There it is, you see ; that is the pity of it. And then you will have to read the books which your husband will choose for you, because when you are married, you will not be able to pretend any more to have read his selections. Really, my poor Alma, I pity you from my very soul."

Alma resented this a little.

" At all events," said Alma, " there will be lots to envy me, and think I'm a luckly girl."

" Those," said Desdemona gravely, " will be the people who do not know what we know. The worst of it is, that Alan is so obstinate. Nothing, for instance, would ever persuade him to bring you up to Weyland Court. He is fixed upon the village life."

" But suppose," said Alma meaningly, " suppose that I were to go over there and say I was going to remain there."

This was rather a facer.

" My dear," said Desdemona, after a pause of a few moments, " that would be impossible, because Weyland Court is let—to the Monks of Thelema."

Then Alma gave way altogether. Her father's scheme, then, was entirely unfeasible. She felt cold and faint.

" It will be quiet for you in the village. Dull, I am afraid. No amusements. Miranda says she will call upon you, but you cannot make yourself happy with an occasional call."

Alma turned white with jealousy — that meaningless jealousy of hers.

" You see," her motherly adviser went on, " I want you to know and understand everything. That is best, to begin with a right understanding, is it not? Well, you can never be to Alan Dunlop what Miranda has been to him. No one can. Had it not been for his philanthropic schemes, he would have certainly married her. She is, indeed, the one woman in the world who knows him thoroughly, and, under other circumstances, ought to be his wife. So, my poor dear, you will have to content yourself with the second place—or, perhaps, as he has many other friends in the Abbey, even with a much lower place in his affections. Of course, he will be personally kind to you. Gentlemen do not beat or swear at their wives."

"You mean," said Alma, her eyes glittering with suppressed fury, "that I am to be nothing in my own house, and that my husband is to think more of Miss Dalmeny than of his wife."

"Why, of course. We all know that. What can one expect, after his long friendship with Miranda? I suppose he has never even pretended to make love to you, my dear?"

"No," replied Alma gloomily; "he never has. He is as cold as an icicle."

"He does not kiss you, I suppose, or say silly things to you, as other men do to their sweethearts?"

She shook her head.

"He has never kissed me. He isn't a bit like other men."

"Dear me! dear me!" sighed Desdemona. "What a dreadful thing to have such a sweetheart! As well have none. And you, too, a girl who knows how men fall in love." Desdemona added this meaningly, and Alma flushed a ruby red. "Did Harry Cardew

ever leave you of an evening without a
kiss ?"

" What do you know about Harry Cardew ?"

" Everything, my dear.   And not only
Harry, but gentlemen, too.   Did not Mr.
Caledon once meet you in the lane and
offer to kiss you ?   Did Mr. Exton take you
through the park that night when you won
the Golden Apple, without the same ceremony ?   My dear, I am a witch ; I know
everything.   You need not try to hide anything from me.   I could tell you the past, and
I can tell you the future.   So you see, Mr.
Dunlop does not love you, else he would kiss
you, just as other gentlemen have done.   Tell
me, my dear child,"—here her voice grew per-
suasive, and she took the girl's hand in her
own soft palm and stroked it—" tell me, do
you *want* to marry him ?"

" No," said Alma, " I don't.   But I must
—I must—cause of father."

" Let me look at the lines of your hand."
Desdemona took the pretty little hand in
hers, and began to examine it curiously.   " I
am a conjurer.   I know all about palmistry.

Um—um—um—this is a very strange hand."

" What is it ?" cried Alma, superstitious, as other maidens be.

" Have you ever had your hand examined by gipsies ?"

" Only once," said Alma, " and it was all nonsense."

" But this is not nonsense. Dear me ! Really ! The most curious thing !"

" Oh ! do tell me," cried Alma.

" My dear, if it had not been for what has happened, you would think I was inventing. Now look at your own hand. What does that line mean across the middle ?"

" I am sure I don't know."

" A marriage interrupted. And what does that line mean under the ball of the thumb ? But, of course, you do not know. A long and happy life. And those lines round the third finger ? Children and grandchildren. My dear, you will be a happy wife and a happy mother ; and yet . . . and yet . . . I do not think it will be in the way you think. I wonder, now, if you have a pack of cards any-where."

" I am sure I don't know."

"There ought to be," said Desdemona, looking about. Presently she opened the drawers of a Japanese cabinet. "Ah! here are some." Alma could hardly be expected to know that she had put them there, arranged for use, that very morning. "Let us see what the cards say."

Alma looked on breathlessly while the con jurer dealt, arranged, and laid her cards in rows, quite after the fashion approved among wise women.

"A brown man," she said, dropping out her sentences as if the cards called for them, "a man with curly hair : a man with rosy cheeks: a tall man : a young man : wedding bells and a wedding ring : a cross : this card looks like a father's anger : this . . . what is this? Your mother does not seem angry. A poor man, too, but riches in the background. My dear, can you explain it all to me?"

"It's Harry Cardew," said Alma eagerly. " It can't be no one else."

"Is it now? You see, my dear, we cannot read names. We can only tell events. And what does all this mean, do you think?

Cards *and* the lines on your hand cannot tell lies, either together or separately."

" I don't know. All I can say is, the banns are up."

" Yes; but there is many a slip, you know. And Harry ?"

" Well . . . but you'll tell Miss Dalmeny."

" Indeed, I will not."

" Then I will try to meet Harry some evening, and ask him can he do anything ? Because, whatever father says, I can't abide the thing, and I won't."

" You are right in one thing, my dear. Have a spirit and a will of your own. I always did say for my own part that a wife should be a man's one thought. Now, there's Miranda and Alan—there they are in the garden at this moment." Alma looked out, and saw them walking over the lawns in eager converse, and her little heart was like to burst with jealousy. " A pretty pair, are they not ? After all, though, it would be a pity to spoil Alan's philanthropic aims, just because he's in love with Miranda."

Alma tossed her head.

" It isn't his philanthropy that I care for,"

she said ; " not one straw.   It's only father,
who wants to get things for himself out of his
son-in-law."

Here, however, the lady they called Desdemona broke off the conversation by sitting
down to the piano and beginning a song.
She had a sweet, strong contralto, and she
knew how to enunciate her words, so that
Alma understood them, and her heart began
to glow within her.

For Desdemona began to sing a song of
a faithful pair of lovers, who were to be
separated by paternal decree and the maiden
given to another ; but that they ran away,
like Keats's young lady, on the very eve of
the wedding, and did not appear again until
Holy Church had fairly made them one.

It was a beautiful song, and sung with the
clear intonation which stage practice gives.
Also, oddly enough, there was a personal
application in the song to her own case, a
thing she had never noticed in hymns, which
were the kind of songs most familiar to
her.

" How should you like, Alma," murmured
the temptress, turning on the piano-stool,

" how should you like to be carried away by
your own true love ?"

" Ah !" said Alma.

" What a splendid revenge !" cried the
actress. She sprang from her feet and began
to act. By what witchery, what enchantment,
did the girl read in the face of the actress, in
her gestures, in her eyes, the whole of a single
scene ? " A revenge indeed. Your father
waiting in the church : your betrothed at the
altar :"—her hands were spread out, her head
erect, her eyes fixed, while Alma bent before
her, mesmerised, unable to lift her gaze from
Desdemona's face, with parted lips and heaving breast—" your bridesmaids wondering
where you are : the clergyman with the book:
the organist tired of playing : the people all
wondering and waiting. Then—a sound of
wheels . . . it is the bride. How beautiful
she looks !—almost as beautiful as you, Alma,
my dear. But she is on the arm of another
man. Heavens ! it is the rival. The people
press and crowd. The men whisper : the
girls laugh and envy her : true love has won
again. You can go, avaricious father—go—
and count your gold." She acted all this

with energy. " You can go, baffled suitor—
you who looked to make your profit out of
the bride you never loved. And you—all
you who pray to see true love rewarded,
come out with us and dance upon the village
green. . . . What a scene! Can you not
picture it? Oh! Alma, Alma, my beautiful
Alma!"

It was a simple trap, but set with the subtlety. Any less direct method would have
roused Alma's suspicions. Now, however,
the simple cottage girl, entranced by this
bewildering picture, intoxicated by Desdemona's praises, overcome by so much sympathy and so much kindness, yielded herself
a ready victim to the actress's blandishments,
and fell into those fat and comfortable arms
and on that ample bosom which lay open and
invited the fond embrace.

CHAPTER III.

"A tall and proper man."

IT was with curiosity that Desdemona awaited
the young gamekeeper, who had taken the
fancy of this village girl. Doubtless, some
clumsy rustic, half a step removed above the
clods of the soil: some bashful, grinning
swain, who might be drawn with his finger in
his mouth, to convey a faithful impression of
his character. Well, she saw a rustic certainly, and yet one of the most magnificent
men she had ever looked upon, the comeliest,
the straightest, and the strongest. His cheeks
were ruddy like David's, his hair was curly
like Absalom's, only he avoided that excessive
length which led to Absalom's untimely end;
his eye as keen as that of the last Mohican.

Desdemona rose out of respect to such
splendid humanity. And then, to the honest

young giant's amazement, she murmured, still
looking at him :

"There be some women, Silvius, had they marked him
In parcels, as I did, would have gone near
To fall in love with him."

And she said aloud,

"Shake hands with me, Mr. Cardew ; I
think you are a very handsome man."

Harry bowed respectfully, but he did not
accept the invitation to shake hands. And
then Desdemona discovered that this handsome man was perfectly self-possessed and
had perfect manners. Her experience of
gamekeepers was naturally small, but her
knowledge of human nature should have
taught her that men who live alone in the
woods, watching the habits of creatures, and
whose work brings them into close contact
with gentlemen, would be likely to acquire a
fine manner.

Harry, then, bowed gravely when this lady
told him he was handsome. He knew the
fact already : he had experienced this kind of
attack on his personal vanity more than once :
but, though it is undoubtedly better to be
good-looking than ugly, good looks will not

keep off poachers, nor will staring at yourself
in a glass keep down vermin. Harry was not
altogether without imagination, but he devoted all his available play of fancy, all that
was imaginative and unpractical in his com-
position, to Alma.

"I wanted to see you," said Desdemona,
"about Alma Bostock."

"About Alma Bostock?"

"I have learned from Mr. Caledon, who
knows you, I believe——"

Harry smiled. "Yes, madam, I know
Mr. Tom very well. Almost as well as I
know Mr. Alan."

"That you and Alma were, until her engagement with Mr. Dunlop, attached to each
other."

"Yes, madam," said Harry quietly; "that
is so. And we are attached still."

"And you hoped to marry her?"

"Surely," said Harry, "surely, we did think
and hope so."

The quiet self-possession of this young
man, and his modest way of answering,
struck Desdemona with a little confusion.

"Pray do not consider me impertinent. I

assure you that I am for many reasons most desirous of helping Alma in this matter."

"No one can help me. Nothing can be done now," said Harry. "Alma's going to marry Mr. Alan, and there's an end."

"And you? What will you do?"

"I shall emigrate," he replied. "I've saved a little money, and I shall go out to Canada."

Desdemona was silent for a while.

"Does Mr. Dunlop know?"

Harry shook his head.

"Unless Alma's told him, he can't know. Because there's only we two, and Mr. Tom Caledon, and now you, who know anything about it."

"Would it not do good to tell him?"

"I think not, madam," replied Harry slowly. "I've turned that thought over in my mind all ways, day and night, to try and get at the right thing; and I've made up my mind that if Mr. Alan hears of it from any one except Alma herself, he'll be set against her, may be, for deceiving of him. Let things be."

"And you have decided to do nothing?"

" Nothing," he said. " There was hope while Alma was at home. I didn't know, but I used to think, when she came out to meet me in the orchard at night, when he was gone, that I should somehow try and find a way. And Mr. Tom, he came and talked it over with me ; but the days went on, and I couldn't hit on any plan. And now, Miss Dalmeny has got her up at the Hall, and will show her the pleasant ways of living like a lady, and fill her head with notions, so as nothing can be done."

" I think that you are wrong ; something may yet be done. Now, Mr. Cardew, what I want to make quite clear to you is that those who love Alma and those who love Mr. Alan —of whom I am sure you are one——"

" Yes," said Harry, " there's no one like Mr. Alan, except Mr. Tom, perhaps."

" All of us, then, have got to do what we can to prevent this marriage."

" But the banns are put up."

" That does not matter. For many reasons, I cannot ask Lord Alwyne, or Miss Dalmeny, or any of the ladies here, to do anything, but I have seen Mr. Caledon, and he will join

me, and we will both work our best for you
to break off the marriage, and you must give
us your help."

Harry looked puzzled.

"You do not understand ? Then let me
explain something. Alma finds out at last
what we have known all along, that Mr. Dunlop wants her to marry him solely in order to
carry out certain plans and theories of his ;
that he means her not to live at Weyland
Court at all, but in a little cottage among the
farm labourers, as he himself has been living,
and to work among them as he has worked.
Stop"—for Harry was about to speak—
"Mr. Dunlop, for his part, believes that she
understands his views, that she will gladly
follow in his steps, and help him with all her
heart to enter into the minds of the villagers,
understand them, and show them the real
Christian life."

Here Harry laughed with derisive pity.

"Alma, for fear of her father, dares say
nothing. Mr. Dunlop, who is, of course, entirely honourable, will keep his engagement,
even if he finds out the truth about her. I
need not tell you that the prospect before

both is of the darkest and most unhappy
kind—for Mr. Dunlop disappointment and
humiliation ; for Alma——"

Here she was silent.

" Yes," said Harry gravely, " I've seen it
all along. For Alma it will be worse."

" Then let us prevent it."

Harry only looked incredulous. How to
prevent a wedding of which the banns were
already put up ? The thing was not in
nature.

" Will you let me tell you a little story ?"

Desdemona told a little story. It was a
story of the same *genre* as that little scene
which she acted for Alma. She acted this as
well, but in a different way, for to Alma she
was melodramatic, exaggerated, exuberant ;
but to this man of finer mould, she was con-
centrated, quiet, and intense. He was not
externally carried away, as Alma. He did not
lean forward with glistening eye and parted
lips, but his cheek grew pale, and his lips
trembled. Indeed, it was a story very much
more to the purpose than any related by
Mr. Barlow to Masters Sandford and Merton.

"And," said Desdemona, coming to an end, "it is not as if we were inviting you to join in a conspiracy against Mr. Dunlop's happiness, or against Alma's. Whatever is the result, so far as Mr. Dunlop is concerned, you will have prevented him from a step which would have ruined his future."

"It seems like a dream," said Harry.

"And perhaps," continued Desdemona, "if those friends so arrange matters as that this wedding does not take place, everybody who knows who those friends were would hold their tongues if necessary."

"Surely," said Harry, "that is the least they could do."

"Then we quite understand ourselves," Desdemona continued. "You will hold yourself in readiness to act some time within the next fortnight. Above all, secresy."

"It seems like a dream," said Harry. "Mr. Dunlop, he'd never forgive me."

"Perhaps not," replied Desdemona; "and if he does not, there are other people in the world. You will not offend Lord Alwyne, I am sure, nor Mr. Tom, nor myself."

Harry stood musing for a little. Then he collected himself.

"I am to see her to-night," he said, "at the end of the garden of the Hall."

"By appointment?" asked Desdemona, a little taken aback—the artful little creature!

"Yes, madam, at her request. What am I to say to her?"

Desdemona could have wished him to tell Alma that she was a cunning and crafty little animal, thus beginning the very first day of her stay with a secret appointment. But she refrained.

"Tell her as little as you can. Only let her know that you alone will be able to stop the marriage, if she keeps quiet and tells no one. And go on meeting her. I will do all I can to make the meetings easier for her and unsuspected by Miss Dalmeny. And now, my friend, good-bye. Shake hands, in token of confidence."

Harry bowed and extended his brown fist with a blush which became him.

"I like you," said Desdemona, "and I will show my liking by giving you an old woman's advice. It is only useful for married men. My advice is no good for bachelors and selfish people like them. Do not, then, begin your married life by thinking your wife an angel. If you do, you will be disappointed. Remember that she is a woman, and though, perhaps, a good deal better than yourself, with a woman's vanities and weaknesses. Remember that. Also, don't humble yourself. Remember that if she has her points, you have yours. And what a woman likes is a husband who rules her; never forget that. She looks for guidance, and if you don't guide her, some other man may. And begin in your home-life as you mean to go on. And do not trust her blindly, because there are some women who go on better if they feel that they are running in harness, with an eye to watch, and a hand upon the rein. One thing more. Remember that all women, like all men, are most easily kept in good temper by praise administered with judgment. Shall you remember all this?"

"I will try," said Harry. "At all events, I see what you mean. Alma isn't a goddess, but I think I can make her into a good wife for me."

Desdemona sat down and considered carefully.

"It cannot be wrong," she thought. "Alan will be cleared of this entanglement. He will marry Miranda. Alma, the poor little, shallow Alma, will marry the man who has fascinated her, and no one will be harmed—except perhaps, that man himself. What a splendid man it is! And he may not be harmed. Alma is not up to his elbow in intellect and goodness ; yet he is strong, and will rule. When a man can rule in his own house, very little harm comes to it. They will all bless and laud continually the name of Desdemona."

And then, her fancy wandering back, she sat for a long time thinking of the past, in which Alan's father was a good deal mixed up.

This was at three in the afternoon. Harry walked across the Park and inspected certain spots where he suspected wires, certain traps where he looked for stoats, killed two vipers, shot a kite, and took other steps in the gamekeeping interests. This brought him to five. Then he made his tea, which took longer in the making than in the drinking.

5—2

Then he took a pipe, and considered with a certain elation, dashed with sorrow, the events of the day. Had his thoughts been written down, they might have taken some such shape as the following : " I am the servant of Mr. Alan, and I am going to take away Mr. Alan's wife that was to have been. But he took away mine that was to have been. And it would be a sin and a shame to let the wedding ever take place. Alma would be wretched, and Mr. Alan disappointed. When he can't marry Alma, he will go back to the young lady he always ought to have married —Miss Dalmeny.

" As for me, Mr. Alan will never forgive me. I shall lose my place, and that is worth a great deal more than I am ever likely to make off a small farm in Canada. But Lord Alwyne will be pleased. One would go a long way to please Lord Alwyne : and him our best friend always, before Mr. Alan came of age. And Mr. Tom will be pleased. One would like to please Mr. Tom. I think that everybody will be pleased.

" Except Bostock. But Bostock has had a whole year's steady run with the Squire, cheating him at every turn, as all the world knows; he ought to be content. I suppose he expected to go on cheating all his life. No, Bostock, you are not going to be the Squire's father-in-law; and it will be worth—well worth Mr. Alan's displeasure to see your rage, when you find the prize slipped out of your fingers, and yourself nothing but bailiff still, with the accounts to make up.

"And as for Alma . . . well . . . Alma is what the Lord made her . . . and if one is in love with Alma, why trouble one's head about Alma's little faults? The lady meant well, no doubt, and gave excellent advice, which if a man would always follow, he'd keep clear of many a pitfall. Poor little Alma!"

All this thinking brought him to half-past eight, and then, mindful of his assignation, he took his gun and strolled leisurely in the direction of the Park. It was half an hour's walk to the garden-gate where Alma was to meet him. Presently, at the point nearest to Weyland Court, there came slowly along in the twilight a pair, hand in hand.

They were Mr. Tom and Miss Nelly, and they looked sad.

Harry took off his hat respectfully.

" Well, Harry," said Tom, putting on a cheerful air, " what news ?"

Nelly went on alone, trailing her parasol in the grass.

" I've seen Mrs. Fanshawe, sir—the lady they call Sister Desdemona."

" Yes—yes."

" And I've come to an understanding with her. I'm to depend on the help of friends, and take the word when the word is given to me."

" All right, Harry, all right. I shall not forget. Have you seen Alma lately ?"

" Not since she came to Dalmeny Hall, sir."

This meant, not for four-and-twenty hours, and Harry hardly thought it necessary to explain that he was on his way to meet her.

" Have you talked it over with her yet ?" Tom went on.

Harry shook his head. Just then Nelly turned back, and joined Tom again.

" Girls," he said, " are girls. That means, begging your pardon, Miss Despard, because I am not talking of ladies, that girls of our

class like admiration and ease, and sitting by
the fire, warm. Therefore, when Mr. Dunlop
asked Alma, she thought at once that he
admired her more than the young ladies of
the Abbey. That turned her brain. And
then she thought it was to be all sitting by
the fire, with her feet on the fender. And
that attracted her too. So that we can't
altogether blame Alma, Mr. Tom."

Harry spoke wistfully, touched his hat, and
went on his way.

Then Nelly, who had been hanging her
head, burst into tears.

"Oh! Tom, every word comes home to
me. *I* like to be chosen out of all the rest.
I like to look forward to a life of ease and
comfort, 'with my feet on the fender.' Oh!
it's shameful—it's shameful. But how to get
out of it. Pity me, Tom."

The "revelations" which Alma made to
her lover were conveyed with the dramatic
energy which characterises young women of
the lower class all over the world, when
narrating their wrongs. She was furious with
everybody : with Miranda for telling her the
truth—"She knew it all along, Harry, and

was only laughing at me in her stand-off way:" with Alan for not telling her before— he had told her dozens of times, only she was not listening: with her mother for rejoicing that her daughter would not be stuck up for the derision of all as a fine lady: with her father for not instantly declaring that the honour of the Bostocks demanded a breaking off of the alliance: with herself for having been so fooled: and, above all, prospectively, with Black Bess for the advantages which this new complication might give her. Nor was her anger appeased at all either by the very hearty kiss which her lover bestowed upon her by way of greeting, nor by that which followed the conclusion of her tirade.

She looked prettier as she stood there, worked up into a royal rage, than even on that night—to be sure Harry was not there— when she stood triumphant before the assembled multitude, bearing round her neck the chain of the Golden Apple. I do not think, now one tries to remember, that an irate Venus has ever been painted. She smiles, she sprawls, she laughs, she leers, she is Venus Victrix, Venus Triumphant, Venus the compeller of hearts, Venus followed by a troop of abject, grovelling men, but she is never, I believe, Venus in a royal rage. And yet, when one thinks of her uncongenial husband, worse for her than Alan Dunlop would be for Alma, one may be sure that there were moments in which her patience gave way, and she sought the relief of attitudes, gestures, and invectives such as one would fain see painted and written. Heavens! What a divine subject—Venus in a Rage! Methinks I see the heaving bosom, the parted lips, the bright and glorious eyes charged with the lightnings of scorn and wrath, the thunders of the brow, the tresses flying in disorder—it is a subject beyond the powers of mortal painter.

"And now, what's to do, Harry?" she asked.

She had exhibited a copiousness of language and a display of imaginative colouring to help out details, in themselves, perhaps, unpromising, which did her infinite credit; and now, her story told, she stood quivering still with her wrath.

"First," said Harry, "first, tell me true—

you were proud that day when Mr. Alan asked you to marry him ?"

" Yes," she replied, " I *was* proud. Wouldn't any girl be proud when the Squire come courting her ? And Miss Miranda and all the beautiful young ladies at the Abbey after him in vain. Why, Harry, it wouldn't be in nature not to be proud, when all the others were made envious."

" And you didn't ask whether he was in love with you ?"

" No, I didn't. He said something about it to begin with, but then—who knows what he says or what he means ? If a man doesn't love a girl, what's the good of his marrying her ?"

" And now you find he doesn't, and you know he wants you for his own experiments, you'd cry off if you could. Think careful what you say, Alma. More depends than you know."

" I would cry off," she replied, " and welcome, only for father. To live in a cottage, and do all the work myself, and have that man with his everlasting talk all day and all night about the house—why—it would be

better to stay at home with father, and that's
not too lively."

"Never mind father," Harry replied
huskily, because this was a very important
question which he was about to put; "never
mind father. Look here, Alma—once for all
—and make an end of it. Will you have me?
No fooling this time."

"What do you mean, Harry?" There was
a light of hope, if not of responsive love, in
Alma's eyes. "Whatever do you mean?"

"I mean what I say. And this time you
must mean what you say. Say No, and I'll
go away and never trouble you nor yours no
more. Say Yes, and we'll laugh at them all
yet."

"But what do you mean, Harry?"

"What I say. Promise to marry me, and
I'll manage it somehow. I shan't tell you
what I'm doing. There shall be no chance
of your letting out secrets. But I'll manage:
I tell you I know how."

"Then, Harry," she said, firmly, "I'll say
Yes, and joyful, if only to get rid of Squire
Sobersides. And now, I suppose," she added,
with a little natural jealousy, "he'll take and

marry Miss Miranda.   Then they can preach
to each other, and much joy may they have."

Clearly Miss Bostock was as yet unfitted
for the professed practice of the Higher Culture.

" And what are you going to do, Harry ?
Won't you tell your own Alma, as loves you
true ?"

By this time the fond gamekeeper had
encircled the waist of this twice-betrothed
nymph.   But he was not to be wheedled.

" Never you mind what I'm doing.   What
you've got to do is just to sit at home, here,
quiet.   You wait patient, and say nothing
till I give the word, and then you do exactly
what I tell you, without letting out a word to
anybody."

" And how will you send me word,
Harry ?"

" By a messenger," he replied mysteri-
ously.   " Never mind who that messenger is.
He'll tell you.   And you may know him, and
you trust him, and do what he tells you."

This was romantic. This was a conspiracy.
Alma felt the delicious excitement of a secret
intrigue creep over her.

" But you've no time to lose, Harry. The banns were up last Sunday, only three weeks before the day."

" Plenty of time. Will you be patient and quiet, even if you don't hear from me till the very day before ?"

She promised again.

" As for your father, we'll make him go round like a bubbling turkey-cock, and as red in the gills. And as for Mr. Dunlop—well —I'm sorry for Mr. Alan. But it's all for his own good," said Harry, cheering up. " He's like David, when he wanted to take away that single ewe lamb of his neighbour's, and the prophet came and prevented of him doing it."

As a gamekeeper, Harry's opportunities of going to church were limited, as everybody knows that Sunday morning is the game-keeper's most busy and anxious time. This fact fully accounts for the curious mess he made of his Bible history.

" Did him good, that prophet," he re-peated.

" Ah ! but, Harry, Mr. Dunlop 'll never for-give you."

" Let him forgive or not, as he likes," said Harry. " We'll go to Canada. I'd as leave go there and farm my own bit o' land, as stay here watching for poachers and destroy-ing of vermin."

"And what will they all say ? Oh—h !" said Alma, with a long sigh of delight at the prospect of assisting in an adventure.

" Folks will talk," said Harry ; "and they may talk about us, if they like, just the same as about other people. Good-night, my pretty. You do just what I say, and heart up."

CHAPTER IV.

"Think women love to match with men,
And not to live so like a saint."

IT was a fact, this engagement, because the banns were put up in church, argued the people. Banns cannot lie. Bostock might very well lie; Alma herself might lie; but banns are not to be disputed. Therefore the country-side became convinced that the Squire of Weyland was really going to marry the Bailiff's daughter, an event as wonderful as that historic parallel of Islington, and the thing could be discussed as if it had already taken place. They knew not, they could not understand, these simple rustics, that the marriage was but a trap set by their Seigneur to catch the sunbeam of their hearts. Had they known that fact they would have regarded the proceeding with the contempt which characterised the prevalent attitude of mind towards the Squire.

" He's not been that good to the village," said the young man they called William, to the cobbler of advanced thought, " as the village had a right to expect from the way he began. They suppers, now, they was good while they lasted—as much beer as you liked, and all—why was they left off ? And the Parliament, where we was to meet and talk, why was that left off ?"

" Meanness," said the cobbler. " Because we wanted to defend our liberties ; ah ! because we wouldn't be put upon with lies no longer ; because some among us wanted to ask questions."

" And the Bar— what call had he to set up a tap ?" asked William. " Who wanted his tap when we'd got our own ? And then made us buy it."

" Gave away the beer, too, at first," growled the cobbler. " They'd make slaves and chains of us all again, they would—him and his lot."

" P'r'aps he'll go back to the Court, now he's married, and let us bide by ourselves,"

said William. " We don't want no Bailiffs'
daughters along of us ; nor no Squires
neither."

" P'r'aps he'll go on as he has a been going
on, corrupting the minds of them as has
otherwise the will to ' read, mark, and in-
wardly digest,' " said the cobbler, thinking of
the Atheistic publications which he had been
unable to procure in the library.

The Bailiff occupied a position so much
higher than their own that the engagement
was not considered in the same light as by
those who stood at Alan's end of the social
ladder. Anything which was likely to remove
this uncomfortable Squire from their midst
was felt to be a relief. Is not that day the
happiest in life when the school-boy steps
forth from the tutelage of masters ? Would
any one like to be always at work under
surveillance ? Why, then, expect it of the
British peasant ?

There was one face, however, which grew
sadder daily, in thinking of the future—the
face of Prudence Driver, the librarian. Alan's
schemes might have failed, but he remained
to her the best and noblest of men, while

Alma Bostock continued to be the shallowest
and vainest of women. This pale-faced little
reader of books knew how to read the natures
of men and women. Not wholly out of her
books, but by mother wit, had she acquired
this power. A man may read and read, and
yet remain a fool. Many do. Prudence
knew Alma, and loved her not; she knew
her antecedents; and she was certain that
the girl would bring her prophet neither help
nor sympathy nor encouragement. And, of
course, she had long known that Alma disliked her, and would perhaps prejudice Mr.
Dunlop against her. Alma might even,
Prudence shuddered to think, cause her to
lose her pleasant place and its sixty pounds
a year. In any case, no more evenings spent
all alone with *him*, while he unfolded his
plans and revealed the manner of life which
he would fain see in his village. No more
would the poor girl's heart glow and her pulse
quicken while he spoke of culture and sweetness spreading through the labourers' cottages.
All that beautiful dream should henceforth be
an impossibility, because Alma would throw
the cold water of indifference on the project.

" I would have," Alan said one night—it was the peroration of a long discourse which he delivered walking about the library, for the instruction of Prudence alone—" I would have the whole day of labour converted into one long poem—a procession of things and thoughts precious and beautiful. The labourer should be reminded at daybreak, as he went forth and watched the mists creep up the hillside, and the trees thereon bathed in the mysterious cloud and sunlight of Turner's landscapes—copies of which he would have studied in our picture gallery; as he stepped along the way, the awaking of life, the twittering of the birds, the crowing of the cocks, should put into his head verses which had been taught him, sung to him, or recited to him at our public evenings. He would shout, then, in his joy. And he would watch the flowers by the wayside with a new and affectionate interest; he would beguile the way with examining the mosses, grasses, and wild vegetation of the hedge; his eyes would be trained for all kinds of observation; he would have a mind awakened to a sense of progress in everything, so that the old conservatism of

6—2

the peasantry, with habit, the rooted enemy
of progress, should be destroyed in him.
He would no longer do the day's work as a
machine, but as an intelligent artist, trying
how it should be done most efficiently. And
on his return, he would find a clean and
bright cottage, a wife who would talk to him
and for him, a meal cooked at our public
kitchen, clean clothes washed at our public
laundry, children taught at our public school,
and nearly every evening something to do,
to hear, to enjoy, which should break the
monotony of the week. Music in every
house; books, joy, and education, where there
is now nothing but squalor, dirt, and beer.
All these things I see before us, Prudence."

Prudence remembered every word. What
part of it would be achieved now, when he
was about to clog his feet with an unsympathetic and indifferent wife? If things were
hard to accomplish before, they would be
tenfold as hard to accomplish in the future.

" Things hard to accomplish ?" Prudence
reflected, with dismay, that as yet nothing had
been accomplished at all, except the general
feeling of discontent. The people did not

want to be meddled with, and Mr. Dunlop appeared to them in the light of a mere meddler and a muddler.

Worse than all this, she saw, she and Miranda alone, that Alan was not happy.

In fact, during the three weeks of publishing the banns, Alan's face grew more sombre every day.

For he felt, though this was a thing he would not acknowledge even to himself, that his marriage would probably be a great mistake.

To feel in this way, even about an ordinary marriage, such a marriage as any couple might contract for their own solace, is indeed a melancholy way of entering upon the holy bond of matrimony; to feel in this way when, as in Alan's case, marriage is intended to advance some great end, is more than melancholy, it is almost desperate. His word was pledged ; he was, therefore, bound to fulfil his part of the contract. And yet . . . and yet . . . it was the wrong woman; he knew it now, it was the wrong woman. Nor was there any other woman in the world with whom he could mate happily, save only Miranda.

When he found Alma alone in the pretty garden, among the rugged old apple-trees, it seemed to him, a dreamer as well as an enthusiast—to be sure, it is impossible to be the one without the other—that the future of things looked rosy and sunshiny. She smiled and nodded, if she did not answer, when he asked her questions; if she did not interrupt him by any questions of her own; if she never showed any impatience to begin her ministrations among the poor, but rather put off his own suggestion that her work in the village homes might be usefully set in hand at once; if she gave him no further insight, as yet, into the minds of the people than he already had—it was, he said to himself, because she was new and strange to the position; that she was as yet only a learner; that she was shy and nervous. He was ready to make all excuses for her—so long as she was at home in her own garden, pretty of her kind, a flower among the common flowers.

At Dalmeny Hall it was different. She sat beside Miranda, and it was like a wild rose beside a camellia, or a daisy beside a tulip, or a russet apple beside a peach. The

face was common compared with Miranda's;
her voice was strident compared with
Miranda's, which was gentle without being
too low; her eyes, bright and animated as
they seemed at her own home, where there
were no others to compare them with, looked
shallow compared with those deep orbs of
Miranda's, the windows of a brain full of
knowledge and noble thought; her expression,
in which could be read clearly, even by Alan,
successive moods of shyness, boredom, and
sullenness, pained and alarmed him. For
what would the future be like, if these things
were obvious in the present? and what should
be done in the dry, if these things were done
in the green?

Miranda did all she could to make the girl
at home and at ease; yet every day saw
Alma more sullen, more silent, more reserved
with her. Perhaps Miranda would have succeeded better had not the custom grown up
during this fortnight of Desdemona seeking
Alma every day, and encouraging her to
confide in her motherly bosom. This Alma
did; she could not help herself; such sympathy was too attractive. At first she trem-

bled, thinking that her confidences would be carried to Miss Dalmeny. But as nothing was carried, she grew more and more unreserved, and finally bared nearly the whole truth. Every day, she confessed, was more irksome to her up in this grand house. She grew tired of wandering about the garden ; she was tired of walking about the rooms ; she could not do work such as ladies do ; she could not play ; she took no interest in books or reading ; she had nothing to talk about with Miss Dalmeny ; she did not care one bit about the things Miss Dalmeny tried to interest her in—cottagers and their ways. And oh ! the dreary evenings when Mr. Dunlop came, looking as if he was going to a funeral; and when he sat with her, or walked with her, talking, talking for ever, as if the more he talked the more likely she would be to understand what had gone before.

But not a word, as yet, to Desdemona of what she had promised Harry.

Then Desdemona, in her warm and sympathetic way, would croon over her, and pat her cheek, telling her how pretty she was, wondering why Alan was so blind to beauty,

commiserating her afresh for the sorrows of
her lot, and holding forth on the obstinacy of
Mr. Dunlop, who, she said, had never been
known to abandon a scheme or confess himself beaten, so that, even when he found that
Alma was not fitted to be the cottagers'
friend, guide, example, and model, as well as
his own servant-of-all-work, he would go on
to the end of his life, or of hers, which
would probably not be a long life, with un-
relenting tenacity of purpose.

Alma shuddered and trembled at the
prospect; and then she thought of Harry
and his promise.

"I'm not married yet," she said, after
Desdemona had exhausted herself in drawing
the gloomy terrors of her future.

"No, my dear," said Desdemona, "no;
that is very true, and yet," she added sorrow-
fully, "the banns have been put up twice, and
there seems no escape for you. What a pity!
what a pity! And you so pretty; and Harry
Cardew such a handsome young fellow.
You'd have made the handsomest couple
ever seen. And Miss Dalmeny would have
taken such a fancy to you, under any other

circumstances. Of course you can't expect her to like you very much now, considering all things."

" No," said Alma, "of course I can't. No girls, not even ladies, like another girl for taking away their sweethearts, I suppose. But I wish mother would let me go home and stay there." She sighed drearily. Even the society of her father seemed more congenial than the frigid atmosphere of Dalmeny Hall.

" Better stay here, my dear," said Desdemona. " Do you know I keep thinking of that line in your hand—the interrupted marriage line; the long and happy wedded life; how can that be? And yet the hand never lies."

With such artful talk did this crafty lady corrupt Alma's simple mind. The girl fell into the trap like a silly wild bird. Fate, she said to herself, ordered her to follow Harry, when he should give the word.

For a fortnight no word came. Then on the Sunday of the third and last publication of the banns, Mr. Caledon met her in the gardens of the Hall. It was in the evening, and Mr. Dunlop was gone. She was think-ing how much she should like to go to the garden-gate and find Harry waiting for her, when she heard a manly heel upon the gravel, and looked up, and in the twilight, saw and knew Tom Caledon.

"I've got a message for you, Alma," he said. "I had to give it to you all alone, with no one in hearing."

"Is it—is it—from Harry?" she asked.

"Yes; it is from Harry. It is a very simple message; I met him to-day, and he asked me to tell you to keep up your heart. That is all."

"Thank you, Mr. Tom." The girl looked humbled. She had lost her old pride of carriage, being every moment made keenly conscious of her inferiority to Miss Dalmeny; and the intrigue in which she was engaged made her guilty and uneasy. Suppose, after all, that Harry should fail. And what did he mean to do?

Alan, for his part, was not without warnings of the future in store for him—warnings, that is, other than his secret misgivings and the pricks of conscience.

He had an anonymous correspondent; a
person apparently of the opposite sex, though
the writing was epicene in character, and
might have belonged to a member of
either sex.

Alan read these letters, which began to
come to him, like many blessings, too late.
Had he acted upon them, indeed, he would
have had to stay the banns after the first
putting up. He felt himself—it was not a
feeling of undisguised pleasure — already
married. The burden of his wife was upon
him. He seemed to have found out, though
as yet he did not put his discovery into
words, that so far from being a helpmeet, she
would become a hindrance ; and that entrance
into the minds of the people appeared to be
as far off as the entrance into Hamath continued to be to the children of Israel.

And so the anonymous letters, some
coming by post, and others pushed under the
door by night, came upon him like a new
scourge. Was it necessary, he thought, that
he should know all the previous life of Alma
—how she had flirted with this man, been
kissed by that, been engaged to a game-

keeper of his own, and had walked through the woods at eve with a Brother of the Abbey?. To be sure, none of the allegations amounted to very much; but when the mind is occupied and agitated these things sting. Again, he might have been foolish in entrusting too much power to a man of whom he only knew that he had been on the point of becoming bankrupt. But what good did it do him to be told that his bailiff was a common cheat and rogue; that he was going to marry the daughter of a man who rendered false accounts, bought cheap and sold dear, and entered the converse in his books; who was notoriously making a long purse out of his transactions for the farm; who was a byword and a proverb for dishonesty and cunning?

These things did no good, but quite the contrary. Alan read them all, cursed the writers, put the letters into the fire, and then brooded over the contents. He would not say anything about them, even to Miranda; an anonymous slanderer is always pretty safe from any kind of punishment; and yet it must be owned that anonymous slanders are

grievous things to receive. Alan read them
and remembered them.

And then little things recurred to him
which he had heard before and forgotten or
taken no heed of. He remembered meeting
Alma one day, when he hardly knew who she
was, walking in a coppice with Harry Cardew,
his old friend and young gamekeeper. Alma
blushed, and Alan, who was thinking about
the grand march of the Higher Culture, just
rashly concluded that here was another case
of rushing into premature wedlock, and went
on his way. Also he had heard Tom
Caledon talking lightly of Alma's beauty, and
thought nothing of it. And now those
anonymous letters accused her of flirting with
half-a-dozen men at once; he would marry a
girl who had been kissed—the writer declared
he had seen the deed perpetrated—by Tom
Caledon, and presumably by his gamekeeper
and a dozen other young fellows. That was
not a pleasant thing to read.

As for the letters, they were written by
one person; he—or she—spelled imperfectly,
and wrote a large and massive hand, covering
a good deal of paper. The letters, like those

of Junius, greatest and most detestable of slanderers, waxed in intensity as they proceeded, until the latest were models of invective and innuendo. The last which came to his hands was dated on the Sunday when the banns had been put up for the third time. It began with the following delicious *morceau.*

"Oh! you pore fool. To think that it's cum to this. You and Alma Bostock called at Church for the third and last time, and after all I've told you. Can't you believe? Then send for Harry, send for Mr. Caledon, if he'll tell the terewth, which isn't likely, being a gentleman; send for Alma's mother, and ast them all, and see what they say. Is it for her looks? Why, she isn't a patch upon the blacksmith's daughter"—could the letter have been written by that young lady? —" not a patch upon her for good looks, and yet you never turned so much as a eye upon her. But you are that blind."

And then the letter proceeded in the usual strain of accusation and libel. Of course Alan was ashamed of reading these things; and still more ashamed of being annoyed by them.

The philosopher, we know, would never be annoyed even by anonymous post-cards, which reflected upon the morals of his female relations and were read by the delighted inhabitants of his kitchen before he received them. The philosopher would rejoice, perhaps, at the thought that cook, housemaid, parlour-maid, and nursery-maid have read these libels, believe in them, will repeat them joyfully, and will exaggerate them.

Alan was probably not a philosopher, because the constant arrival of these letters did not make his countenance more cheerful when he went up to see Alma in the evening.

His gloom communicated itself to Miranda. She found it hard any longer to believe in a girl who could not cultivate enthusiasm for Alan. She was dejected and unhappy. She went little to the Abbey during these weeks; she lost interest in the place wherein she was wont to delight. Her cheek grew pale and her eyes heavy. She was kind to Alma, but she ceased her endeavours to interest her in the things which her husband would look for. Alma, for her part, became sullen and silent, restless in the house, and restless in the garden, where she walked for hours. She did not go again to the farm, and when her mother came, received her with a coldness which was worse than any of her ancient insubordination. Desdemona alone preserved a demeanour of cheerfulness even beyond that to which her friends were accustomed to see in her.

Therefore, during these three weeks when the banns were being published, and while the man and the woman about to take upon themselves indissoluble and lifelong vows should have been growing to know each other more and more, they were drifting apart. Alan was every day more sombre, colder, more of a schoolmaster, and less of a lover. Alma every day, more silent, less prodigal of her smiles, more reserved, and—a thing patent to her *fiancé* and of very unpleasing omen—more sullen.

CHAPTER V.

"There's nought in this bad world like sympathy;
 'Tis so becoming to the soul and face;
Sets to soft music the harmonious sigh,
 And robes sweet friendship in a Brussels lace."

MEANTIME, there seemed, to Desdemona's observant eyes, to be growing up in the Abbey a kind of restlessness. Unquiet betokens change. Was it, she asked, that the Monks and Sisters were tired of the Abbey or of each other? No; she made inquiries, and found that the general feeling was quite in the contrary direction. The place appeared to them still a most delightful haven. Yet there was a certain sadness prevalent. Could this melancholy be a contagious disorder taken from one or two afflicted members? Nelly, for instance, had obviously been

pale of face and sad of aspect for some time
past. She seemed to take a comparatively
feeble interest in the matter of dress; she
was known on more than one occasion to
shut herself up alone in her own cell for
hours; her delight in riding, dancing, talking,
acting, singing, lawn-tennis, and all the pleasures in which she was once foremost, was no
longer what it had been. Doubtless, in her
case, the cause was in some way to be attributed to Tom Caledon. They must have
quarrelled; otherwise, why did they avoid
each other? Why did they look at each
other guiltily, as people do who have a secret
between them? To be sure, Desdemona
could not know the nature of that admonition
which Tom pronounced after the Court of
Love. And that was all their secret.

As for Tom Caledon himself, he too was
grown melancholy. In these bad days he
mooned—he who had been the most com-
panionable of men, who had ever fled from
the solitude of self as eagerly as any mur-
derer of ancient story—he who was formerly
never out of spirits, never tired of laughing
with those who laughed, and singing, meta-

phorically, with those who sang, was grown
as melancholy as Jaques in the Forest of
Arden.

" Perhaps," said Desdemona—she was
sitting in her own capacious cell, and
Miranda was with her; Mr. Paul Rondelet
was also with them—he was seen a good deal
with Miranda during these days—" Perhaps,
Miranda, the presence of two perpetually wet
blankets, such as Tom and Nelly, has imper-
ceptibly saddened our refectory and drawing-
room.   Blankets which *will* not dry, however
long you hang them out, would sadden even
the Laundry of Momus."

Paul Rondelet was leaning against the
mantelshelf, a position which he affected because—he was no more free from personal
vanity than yourself, my readers, although so
advanced in thought—it showed to advantage
his slender figure, and allowed the folds of
the tightly-buttoned frock which he always
wore to fall gracefully.   He looked up lan-
guidly, and began to stroke his smooth cheek
with great sadness, while he let fall from an
overcharged soul the following utterance:

" Momus is the only one of the gods who

is distinctly vulgar. How depressing is mirth!
How degrading it is to watch a laughing
audience—a mere mob with uncontrolled
facial muscles! Momus is the god of music-
halls."

"Cheerfulness is not mirth," said Miranda
quietly; "but you are sad yourself, Desdemona."

"I am," she replied, clasping her hands,
"I am. It is quite true; I am encumbered
with my Third Act."

"And I," said Miranda the straightforward,
"am sad for Alan's sake."

"But you, Mr. Rondelet"—Desdemona
turned to the Thinker, whom she loved at all
times to bring out—"you, too, are melancholy. You neglect your monastic vows;
you seldom appear at the refectory; you contribute nothing to the general happiness; you
are visible at times, walking by yourself, with
knitted brows. Is this to be explained?"

Paul Rondelet lifted his white brow and
played with his eye-glass, and sighed. Then
he gazed for a moment at Miranda.

Had he told the exact truth, he would have
confessed that his debts worried him, that his

anxiety about the future was very great. In fact, that he was entirely absorbed in the worry of his duns and the trouble of having no income at all in the immediate future. But he did not tell the truth. When facts are vulgar, truth-seekers like Paul Rondelet avoid them.

"The conduct of life," he said grandly, "is a problem so vast, so momentous, that there is not always room for pleasant frivolities, even for those of this little society. These are the trifles of a vacation. When serious thoughts obtrude themselves——"

"I see," said Desdemona, interrupting ruthlessly. "Why not write them down, and have done with them?"

Paul Rondelet shook his head.

"You are accustomed to interpret men's thoughts," he said, "you can give life and action to words ; but you do not know by what mental efforts—what agonies of travail —those words were produced."

"Perhaps not," said Desdemona most unfeelingly. "I suppose small men suffer in their attempt to say things well. Shakespeare,

Shelley, and Byron do not seem to have endured these throes."

Small men! Oh, this fatal lack of appreciation!

There was a cloud upon the whole Abbey. The sadness was not confined to the three or four named above ; it was, with one exception, general. While Nelly lingered alone in her cell, while Tom Caledon rode or walked moodily in the lanes, while Mr. Paul Rondelet was seen to go alone with agitated steps, so that those who beheld thought that he was grappling with some new and brilliant thing in verse, the whole fraternity seemed drifting into a constrained self-consciousness most foreign to the character of the Order. Nobody now went off in happy solitude to lecture an empty hall; the three journals of the Abbey appeared at more irregular intervals; Cecilia gave no concerts ; nobody translated a new play; nobody invented a new amusement. Instead of general conversation, there was a marked tendency to go about in pairs. And when there was any singing at all, which was not every evening, as of old, it generally took the form of a duet.

What had befallen the Abbey?

There was, as I have said, one exception: Brother Peregrine alone was cheerful. Nothing ever interfered with a cheerfulness which at this juncture was unsympathetic; neither rainy weather, nor the general depression of the Brethren, nor even the sadness of Nelly, whom he continued to follow like a shadow. And yet, though he was always with her, though the Sisters wondered whether Nelly had accepted him, and while she wondered why he was silent, Brother Peregrine had not spoken the expected words.

To the rest it seemed as if the Court of Love, the Judgment of Paris, and all their masques, sports, dances, and entertainments, were become part and parcel of a happy past which would never return again. Brother Peregrine alone was the same as he had always been. He alone was unconscious of the general discontent. This was due to his eminently unsympathetic character. He came to the Abbey with the purely selfish design of getting as much pleasure out of so novel a society as possible. He got a great deal. When he told stories, or did Indian tricks, or

performed feats on horseback, which he had
learned in India, the Sisters of the Order
laughed and applauded; it was he who devised pageants, suggested things to Desdemona, and improved on her ideas. Thus the
Judgment of Paris was his doing, and he
acted, as we know, as Sister Rosalind's counsel
in the Court of Love. While he could bask
in the sunlight of fair eyes, delight in the
music of girls' laughter, drink good wine, sit
at feasts, listen to music, and be himself an
active part in the promotion of all modern
forms of conviviality, he was happy. He was
exactly like the illustrious Panurge, in one
respect, in being entirely without sympathy.
You knew him, therefore, as well the first day
as the fiftieth; there was nothing to be got
out of him except what he offered at first.
Had he put his creed into words, it would
have been something like this : "Everybody
wants to enjoy life. I *mean* to, whether other
people do or not; I take whatever good the
gods send, and mean to use it for myself; if
people wrong me, or annoy me by suffering,
pain, or complaint, I go away, or else I take
no notice of them."

The Abbey was an excellent place for such a man, because in no other place were the ways of life so smooth. And a man of such a temperament would be very long in discovering what Desdemona, with her quick sympathies, felt as soon as it began—the growing constraint.

For, of course, the Brethren and the Sisters were not going to sit down and cry or sulk, as is the wont of the outer world. There was neither growling nor grumbling in the Abbey, unless it were in each member's cell. Brother Peregrine noted nothing, because there was no outward change. If Nelly's cheek was pale, she listened to him still, and he followed her as before. If the Order, generally, was depressed, there were still the functions—guest night, choral night, theatre, concert, dancing, all were duly celebrated. The Lady Abbess presided at the refectory, Desdemona performed her duties as directress of ceremonies, and the only difference was that the sparkle had gone out of the wine— it was gone flat. This they all perceived, except Brother Peregrine, who still thought the goblet as *mousseux* and as brilliant as before. The climax was reached when they attempted one of their old costume balls, which had been a sort of *spécialité* of the Abbey. They got as many guests to fill their rooms as they could bring together; but —it was not possible to disguise the truth— it fell flat. The guests went away early; there was little spirit in the dancing; and the chief actors who ought to have thrown life into it —the Monks and Sisters—were languid.

Next evening, after dinner, when they were all collected in the drawing-room, Desdemona lifted up her voice, and asked tearfully:

"What is it, children? Is the wine of life already run down to the lees?"

No one answered, but the Sisters gathered round her as if they looked to her for help.

"Are there no more cakes and ale?" she went on. "Everything fails. Can the Abbey —our Abbey of Thelema—be a failure?"

"No—no," they declared unanimously.

"Are you happy here, my dears?" she asked the Sisters.

They looked at one another, blushed with one consent for some reason of their own unexplained, and then murmured that they had never been so happy before, and never could be happier in the future.

Brother Peregrine remarked that he himself felt perfectly, monastically happy. Indeed, he looked it, standing before them all, with his thin figure, his complacent smile, and his wonderful absence of any appreciation of the situation. Under any circumstances, if Brother Peregrine himself had no personal care he would have looked equally happy.

Desdemona contemplated him with a little wonder. Was the man perfectly self-contained? Even Paul Rondelet's philosophy of separation did not rise to these heights of blindness.

"If you are perfectly happy," said Desdemona sharply, "you are not monastically happy. Perhaps, on the other hand, you deserve to be pitied."

"Let us invent something," said Peregrine cheerfully, as if a fillip of that kind would restore happiness, just as certain ladies fly to little suppers with something hot in order to soothe the wounded spirit. "Has everybody lectured?" He looked round radiantly, conveying his belief that a lecture was the one thing wanting.

No one would hear of lectures.

"I have learned a new conjuring trick," he went on. "Would you like to see that?"

"I think," said Desdemona, "that the present situation will not be improved by tricks."

"When the knights and ladies of the middle ages," Brother Peregrine went on, nothing daunted, "were shut up in their castles for the winter, they used to amuse themselves——"

"*Moult tristement*," said Desdemona.

"With games. Sometimes they played hot-cockles, the laws of which I dare say we could recover if we tried; or blind man's buff, which you would perhaps rather not play; or touch me last, which I can fancy might be made as graceful a pastime as lawn tennis. Then there was the game of *gabe*, at which everybody tried to out-brag everybody else; and the favourite game of *le roy ne ment pas*, at which everybody had to answer truthfully whatever questions were asked. There were to be no reservations; the answers were to be absolutely truthful."

"I should think," said Desdemona, "that your games must have been almost maddening in their stupidity. I would as soon suggest to the Abbey that we should amuse ourselves at *bouts rimés.* Will you play something, Cecilia ?"

She went to the piano and began to play some melancholy yearning music, such as might fall upon sad souls with a sympathetic strain. Desdemona listened and reflected. All this dejection and constraint could not arise from disgust at Brother Hamlet's madness, or from sympathy with Tom Caledon. Sympathy there was, no doubt. Everybody liked Tom. Disgust there was, no doubt. Everybody was indignant with Alan. But that all the springs of joy should be devoured by the disappointment of one Brother, and the crotchets of another, seemed absurd.

And suddenly a thought came into her mind. Desdemona caught it and smiled. Then she looked round the room and smiled again. Cecilia was playing her melancholy music : the Sisters were listening, pensive; the Brothers stood or sat about among them in silence. Tom Caledon was in one window, looking gloomily upon the twilight garden ; Nelly was in another, pulling a rose to pieces.

On the faces of all, except of two, there was
in different degrees a similar expression, one
of constraint, perhaps of impatience, and
perhaps of hope.

Of course the two exceptions were Brother
Peregrine and Paul Rondelet. When the
former, who had no taste for music, was cut
short by Desdemona, he retreated to a table
at the other end of the long room, where,
with a perfectly happy face, he found a book
of burlesques, and read it with appreciation.
Paul Rondelet entered the drawing-room just
as Cecilia began to play. He, too, having
no real ear for music, though he talked much
of the Higher Music, and held Wagner among
his gods, retired to the same part of the room
as the Brother whom most he disliked.
Here he found Mr. Pater's volume on the
Renaissance, with which while the following
scene was enacted, he refreshed his soul.

"As for Peregrine," said Desdemona to
herself, looking at his perfectly happy and
perfectly unsympathetic face, "that man may
have escaped from some great unhappiness,
such as a convict's prison, or something as
bad, so that everything else seems joy; or he

may be a perfectly selfish person, incapable of seeing beyond the outward forms, or—which I hope is not the case—he may have secured Nelly, and so chuckles easily over his own future."

Then she looked at the other man. Either Mr. Pater had made some remark, which displeased Paul Rondelet, or he was thinking of something unpleasant, unconnected with that author. "As for that man," thought Desdemona, "there is something wrong with him. To be sure, he never ought to have been a Monk at all. He has an anxious look. Perhaps he is in debt. It requires a man of a much higher stamp than that poor fellow to bear up against debt. Or some one may have derided his poetry."

It will be seen that Desdemona was not very far wrong in any of her conjectures. But then she was a witch, a sorceress.

"As for the rest," she continued to herself, "they are all afflicted with the same malady. It is not *ennui*, it is not boredom, it is not anxiety. What can it be but one thing?"

And, as before, the sweetest and most gratified of smiles played about her comely face.

"Of course," she said aloud, so that all started, "I knew it would come, sooner or later. At least, I ought to have known, but did not think, being quite a stupid old woman. And now it has come."

"What *do* you mean, dear Desdemona?" asked Cecilia, stopping her music.

"My dear," said Desdemona, "be good enough to stop that melancholy strain, which only expresses your own mood, and perhaps that of a few others, but not mine at all. I am an outsider, by reason of age and experience. Will you play for me only, and for nobody else, a grand triumphal march?"

Cecilia obeyed, and straightway the air was filled with the trumpet-notes of triumph, the rejoicings of a multitude, the hymns of those who praise, and the shouts of those who offer thanks. Presently the hearts of the pensive Sisterhood rose with the music; soft eyes brightened; closed lips parted; drooping heads were uplifted. When Desdemona presently looked round, Tom Caledon had joined Nelly in her window, and both looked happy. The Brothers and the Sisters were in groups and pairs. Only there was a change, she thought, because there was a touch of solemnity in all the masculine eyes, and of a certain veiled and happy triumph under the drooping feminine lids, as if this was no ordinary evening. Brother Peregrine, unmoved by the exultation, as he had been by the melancholy of the music, sat cheerfully smiling over his odd volume of burlesques. So, too, unmoved by music of despondency or triumph, sat the disciple of Wagner and the Higher Music, Mr. Paul Rondelet, brooding over his cares. Music had no charms to make him forget his duns.

The music stopped with a final rapture, as if human joy could no further find expression.

Desdemona began, then, the speech, which more than anything else has endeared her to the hearts of those who listened. She had ever been the guiding spirit of the Abbey. It was she, we know, who invented their pageants and varied their entertainments. It was she who delighted the girls with her wisdom, her experience, and her sympathy. It was she who took care that the right Brother was told off for the right Sister; it was she who on occasion knew, better than any one, even better than Miranda, how to throw such a spirit into the Abbey as prevented it from becoming a mere place of idle amusement. To her they owed everything. But after this evening they agreed that their previous debt of gratitude was multiplied tenfold, and that they were bankrupt, one and all, in thanks. At least everybody said so, except Paul Rondelet and Brother Peregrine.

"The Abbey of Thelema, my dear Sisters," this benevolent person began, comfortably leaning back in the softest of armchairs, her feet upon a footstool, her hands clasped comfortably in her lap, her face just within the light of a shaded lamp, while two or three of the Sisters were lying at her feet, and the rest were grouped round her, and while the Brothers inclined a respectful ear— " The Abbey of Thelema was constituted to contain no Sisters but such as were young, comely, of good birth, and gracious manners. So far, with the exception of one, who is but a servant of the rest and an elderly woman— myself, my dears—the intentions of the Founder have been strictly carried out. I

8—2

would he were here to-day in person to see how fair to look upon, and how gracious of demeanour, are the present Sisters of Thelema. And it was to contain no Monks but such as were also young, well bred, and of good repute. The Brothers are older at admission than they were at the first foundation, just as the undergraduates of the Universities are older at admission than they were five hundred years ago. Also the first Abbey was designed as the school of gentlehood ; ours is an Abbey in which, like that of Fontévrault, the Monks and Sisters are already trained in the ways of the gentle life. But I wish that the Founder were here to-day to see what a goodly assemblage of Brothers we have to carry out his intentions. The Monks and Nuns of the old Thelema, as of ours, were to be bound by no conventual fetters ; so far from that, as you know, they were bound to respect the vows which other Monks and Nuns officially deride. It was even contemplated by the Founder that the unrestrained society of knightly youth and gentle demoiselle would inevitably result—in honourable love; and he showed in his dream

how they would go forth as from a sacred
Ark, in pairs, to spread · throughout the
world the blessings of gentleness and good-
breeding."

Here Desdemona stopped, conscious of
a "sensation" among her audience. She
lowered the light at her elbow, and the dis-
creet Tom Caledon, who, with Nelly, had
joined the group and was now listening,
thoughtfully lowered another lamp, which
stood on a table at hand. Then there was
a soft religious light, except at the other
end of the long drawing-room, where Brother
Peregrine was still chuckling over his bur-
lesque, and Mr. Paul Rondelet was still
grinding his teeth over his private troubles,
or else over Mr. Pater's sweet and intelligible
English.

"My children," Desdemona went on, in a
lowered voice, "I have seen what has fallen
upon this Abbey. Why should we hope
to escape what, in his great wisdom, our
Founder foresaw would happen ? What have
we done that we should go on prolonging
indefinitely the simple joys which belong to
the play-time of life ? In all our pageants

and in all our pleasures we have but been playing at happiness ; preparing for the future as a schoolboy prepares himself in the playing-field for the battle-field. I think that this your play time, and my great joy as one of the audience, is nearly over : I think that it is time to bring it to a close. Not altogether : other Abbeys of Thelema will be raised for other Monks and Sisters ; we shall remain friends, and meet and greet each other ; but ours, in its old form, will soon be as a memory."

No one spoke in reply.

" Tell me, dear Sisters—nay, dear children —that all is as it should be. There are no jealousies in the Abbey ?"

" None," they murmured.

" Then the will of the Founder has been fairly carried out, and we may prophesy the closing of our Abbey with joy and congratulation. Tell me when you like, and as much as you like, to-morrow, my children. To-night we will have cheerful looks and happy hearts again, though the play is well-nigh finished."

She raised the light again. Tom disen-

gaged his hands—what was it held them ?—
and turned up his lamp.

"To-day is Tuesday," said Desdemona,
rising. "I announce a solemn banquet, a guest
night, a choral night, a full-dress monastic
night, for Saturday. I believe there will be
no dancing, or singing, or any other amusement at all that day. Let us have as many
guests as we can muster."

"But it is the day of Alan's wedding,"
said Miranda.

"My dear Miranda," Desdemona replied,
with the slightest touch of asperity, " I have
several times observed that Alan is not
married yet."

" It is the day," said Nelly, "when mamma
wishes me to return to Chester Square."

"My dear Nelly," said Desdemona, still
with asperity, "do not make difficulties.
You have not gone to Chester Square yet.
Perhaps you will not go on that day at all."

There was an inharmonious chuckle from
the other end of the room. Brother Peregrine had come to a very funny part. It
seemed as if he was chuckling in reply to
Desdemona.

Nelly looked at him and shuddered ; but no one spoke.

" On Saturday," Desdemona went on, " we will have a full meeting, even if it be our last. Till then, my children, be happy with each other."

Cecilia took her zither and touched the chords.

" May I sing," she asked, " the ' Rondeau of the Land of Cocaigne' ? " It was prophetic of the Abbey of Thelema.

" In the land of Cocaigne, where travellers tell,
All delights and merriments dwell,
Love, and joy, and music, and mirth,
Loss of trouble, and lack of dearth—
There I found me a magic well,
Deep in the greenest depths of a dell,
Lined with moss, and edged with shell,
Precious above all springs of the earth,
In the land of Cocaigne.
I drank of the waters ; straight there fell
Behind me, each with the clang of a knell,
The days of grief: Love sprang to birth,
Laden with gifts of gladness and worth,
And singing a song of a wedding-bell
In the land of Cocaigne."

CHAPTER VI.

"She is a woman, therefore may be wooed."

IF the other Brothers of the Order were contemplating marriage with the ardour of lovers, Mr. Paul Rondelet was considering that condition of life, as calmly as his creditors would allow him, as a haven of refuge. His position was really unequalled in history. Addison, to be sure, endured a temporary period of poverty; but Paul Rondelet was about to face destitution. In another short half year he would be without an income—absolutely without any money at all; already every other post brought letters from once trustful tradesmen, some openly threatening, some darkly hinting at legal proceedings. Think of the absurdity of the thing. A man actually in the very

van and forefront of modern culture : a man
with a following of his own : a leading member of the Advanced School : a man so
exalted above his fellows that he could afford
to feel pity, a gentle pity—not contempt or
exasperation at all — with those who still
believed in Christianity, patriotism, the old
ideas about poetry or art : a man so skilled
in the jargon of Art criticism, that people
forgot to ask whether he knew a good picture
when he saw one, and accepted on his dictum
lean and skinny women, with red hair and sad
faces, as the highest flights of modern art; so
apt with the jargon of modern poetic criticism,
that people only gasped and supposed that,
after all, knock-kneed spasms of unreal rapture or crack-jaw dithyrambs, where nonsense
pretended to be profundity incapable of
articulate speech—was the real, and hitherto
undiscovered poetry—so apt, also, with the
latest book jargon, that it required a cool head
to discover that he seldom read a new book
at all.   Such a man was positively going out
into the cold and unsympathetic world without
an income.

England is not like the East : you cannot

wander from village to village, another Mo-
hammed, with your following of listeners,
living on the dates, rice, pillau, olives, figs,
and bread, offered freely to all travellers ; nor
is it like that France of six hundred years
ago, when an Abelard could retire into the
country and pitch a philosophic tent, surrounded by thirty thousand disciples.

Faint thoughts did cross the mind of Paul
Rondelet that he, too, might set up his own
lecture tent, say on Salisbury Plain, whither
the undergraduates might flock, for the sake
of the Higher Culture. But no : it was a
dream—a dream.

It was already three weeks since he first
made up his mind that Miranda should be
his wife ; since, in fact, he heard that Alan
was resolved upon his matrimonial suicide.
There were, most certainly, other Sisters in
the Abbey desirable for beauty, and not wholly
destitute of culture or of money. But Miranda
alone seemed to this leader of modern thought
wholly worthy to wear his name. She appeared to appreciate him, which he felt could
not be said of all the other ladies ; she was
undeniably beautiful ; she was possessed of

many broad acres. Her beauty was of a kind
which Paul Rondelet felt he would admire
more in his own wife than in other people's.
For it was not the beauty lauded by his own
school. She was not lithe, lissom, and ser-
pentine : she had none of the grace of the
leopardess about her : her eye was lit by
no baleful fires of passion : she was not skinny
or bony : she did not writhe as she walked :
she was not sad-avised : nor was her hair
like unto that of the painted dames in the
Grosvenor Gallery, or of the yellow-haired
Somanli who greets the traveller at Aden ;
it was not yellow tow at all. And in dress
she made fashion her slave instead of her
mistress. She was not, in short, either in
appearance, in dress, or in manner, at all like
unto the self-conscious young woman who
follows the newest fashions of self-conscious
and priggish modern art. Paul Rondelet felt
that he should be proud of her. It must be
said of him, the Master, the Poet, the man
of taste, the Prophet of Higher Culture, the
fastidious Paul Rondelet, before whose deci-
sions, as his school considered, artists trembled,
that he had chosen a companion worthy of
himself.

Above all things, the man of Higher Culture is a critic. As his wines, his engravings, his chairs, his bookbinding, his water-colours, his dinners, his little Sunday morning breakfasts, must all be perfect, so must his wife be perfect. Now, Paul Rondelet felt that he could visit Oxford proudly with Miranda, or, better still, make of Dalmeny Hall a perfect home, an improved Oxford, a college without the uncongenial element.

He went over to the house in order to examine for himself its capabilities. True, it was not like Weyland Court—very few houses are—but still there were great things to be done with Dalmeny Hall, by one who knew how to work. Two or three rooms, he thought, would lend themselves with peculiar readiness to the modern Nobler Treatment. One might even be converted into a peacock-room. All of them, with right paper, right fireplaces, right cabinets, right china, right Harmonies in Blue or Brown, right chairs and right tables, might be converted into apartments, in which even the most advanced would find pleasure. Life, he thought, might be made philosophically perfect at Dalmeny Hall. Certain modifications would be made : he could not allow Desdemona, a person who pretended to no sympathy with him or his school, to consider, as she did at present, the house her own. Miranda herself would require in some respects a certain amount of moulding before she became perfectly imbued with the newest ideas. It was unfortunate for her, he considered, that Alan Dunlop, who had exercised so great an influence over her, left Oxford before the opinions of the school arrived at their full development ; that is to say, before they quite grasped the doctrines that patriotism is a mark of Philistinism—the true country of every philosopher being the world—religion a pitiable survival of the dark ages : all the art, architecture, music, and poetry of the last three hundred years—except, perhaps, the architecture of Queen Anne—a wretched exhibition of ignorance, bad taste, and vulgarity. When Alan went away they had only arrived at the stage of looking on whatever pleases the majority of mankind with contempt, pity, and suspicion.

But he should mould her : he should be

able, through her very admiration of himself, to inspire a desire for higher levels of thought. Together, while poor Alan, mated to his rustic beauty, worked his heart out in a hopeless endeavour, they too, he thought, should present to high and low, the admirable spectacle of the perfect Olympian life.

It was difficult to get an opportunity of finding Miranda alone. Paul Rondelet—I think I have remarked that all the members of his school spoke of him as Paul Rondelet, not as Rondelet, or Mr. Rondelet, but plain Paul, as one speaks of Burne, Jones, Julius Cæsar, and other illustrious men—sought in vain for many following days. It was partly that quest of an opportunity which drove him to wander ceaselessly in the gardens, in the courts of the Abbey, and in the park between Weyland Court and Dalmeny Hall. Desdemona, who watched everything, marked his uncertain steps and wondered.

" Another trouble," said Miranda to Desdemona, but she did not look troubled.

" What is it, dear ?"

" It is Mr. Rondelet," she replied calmly. " He is going to offer me his hand."

"My dear Miranda!" Desdemona cried, in some alarm. "Pray, be careful. He is a young man to whom it will be necessary to speak very plainly. But you may be mistaken."

"Not at all, I am quite sure. Remember that I have had experience. It interests me a good deal now to watch the beginnings of these things."

Miranda sat down, and went on with her experience.

"I grew to discern their intentions almost as soon as they formed the idea in their own minds. Then I used to study the development, and when the time came, I was perfectly prepared with my answer. And I cannot be mistaken in Mr. Rondelet. All he wants is an opportunity."

"And will you give him one?"

"I think I must. It is always better to get these things over. Poor Mr. Rondelet! I dare say he spared me out of consideration to Alan, until that—that engagement. It was good of him."

"It would have been better to have spared you altogether."

" My dear, Mr. Rondelet is poor, and I am rich," said Miranda. " He shall have his opportunity."

In fact, she gave him an opportunity the very next day.

He found her in her own garden alone. Alma had been with her, unwilling, and had just escaped, leaving Miranda saddened at the hopelessness of getting at the better side of the girl, who continued to remain dull, apathetic, and reserved. In fact, she was thinking, day and night, of nothing but the splendid *tour de force* which Harry was about to perform for her deliverance. The knowledge of this coming event enabled her to be less careful about hiding her discontent and sulkiness, so that she was by no means an agreeable companion.

When Paul Rondelet came upon Miranda, there was a look of languor and fatigue in her face, but her cheek brightened with a quick flush when she saw him walking delicately across the grass, putting up and dropping his eye-glass. Her eyes lit up, but her lips set themselves firm—she was going to hear and to reply to a proposal, unless, as had happened in other cases, he would, at the last moment, become nervous.

Such was not Paul Rondelet's intention. He had been looking at the case to himself, for some days past, from as many points of view as Mr. Browning loves to contemplate a murder. It would be said that he married for money. To be sure, had Dalmeny Hall belonged to himself, he would not have fettered himself with a wife. His school do not greatly love matrimony; on the other hand, he might fairly urge that he brought his wife a fair equivalent for her fortune; and though he was not her equal either in birth—his grandfather belonged to the pre-historic period, and was only conjectural—or in wealth, he was a leader in the most advanced school of Oxford. If Oxford, as all true Oxonians believe, and would suffer lingering tortures rather than give up, leads the thought of the world, then, confessedly, Lothian leads Oxford, and Paul Rondelet led, or thought he led, Lothian. Therefore, Paul Rondelet led the world.

"You may have observed, Miss Dalmeny" —Miranda noticed that there was not a bit of love in his face—"You may have observed"—here he let fall his eye glass, and put it up twice—"that I have of late endeavoured to convey to you an idea of the feelings which . . . which . . ."

"Not at all," said Miranda, untruthfully. "Pray sit down, Mr. Rondelet, and tell me what you mean."

"Let me," he said, sitting down at one end of the garden-seat, Miranda occupying the other; "let me put the case from our own—I mean, the Higher Modern—point of view. Our school have arrived at this theory, that it is useless and even mischievous to attempt to promote culture. Especially is it mischievous when such efforts lead to personally interesting oneself with the lower classes. They are led, among other things, to believe that they are not entirely deserving of scorn. Therefore, we have decided on a return to the principles of the Renaissance."

"Really," said Miranda, looking at him with a little amusement in her eyes. This infinite condescension at the same time irritated her.

"Our plan of life is—separation. We

9—2

leave the vulgar herd entirely to themselves ;
and we live alone, among our own set, on our
own level."

"Will not that be very dull? Should
you admit the Monks and Sisters of
Thelema ?"

Paul Rondelet hesitated, and dropped his
glass; then he replaced it with a sigh. "I
fear not. Perhaps one or two. But, Miss
Dalmeny, the higher life cannot be dull. It
has too many resources. It is great, though
perhaps the vulgar cannot know its greatness;
it is memorable and precious, though it is
spent apart from mankind. We care nothing
about our reputation among men. We belong
to the lower levels in no way—the poor may
help the poor, we shall not help them at all,
or vex our souls about them. We are no
longer English, or French, or Russian, or
German ; we are no longer Catholics or
Anglicans, or anything ; we propose to divest
ourselves of any, even the slightest, interest
in their religions, their politics, or their aims ;
we are alone among ourselves, the Higher
Humanity."

"Oh !" said Miranda again. "And what

are we, then? I always thought, in my conceit, that I belonged by birth and education to the Higher Humanity."

Paul Rondelet shook his head sadly.

"Alas! no," he said; "I would that we could acknowledge your right to rank with Us. It is not a matter of birth, but one of culture. The Higher Humanity consists entirely of the best intellects trained in the best school. The men can only, therefore, be Oxford men, and presumably of Lothian."

"And the women—oh! Mr. Rondelet—I should so much like to see the women of the Higher Humanity."

Was she laughing at him, or was this genuine enthusiasm?

"The women," he said, "either the wives of the men, or their disciples, must be trained by the men."

"And must they, too, be great scholars?"

"Nay," he replied kindly. "What we look for in women is the Higher Receptivity"—it really was exasperating that Paul Rondelet wanted everything of the Higher order—"The Higher Receptivity, coupled with real and natural taste, hatred for debasement, especially in Art, a love for Form, an eye for the Beautiful, and a positive ardour to rise above prejudice. One of us was recently engaged, for instance, to a lady who seemed in every way adapted for his wife . . ."

"Was he a leader in the Advanced School?"

"He was a— a—, in fact, one of the leaders." Paul Rondelet spoke as if there was in reality one leader only—himself. "After training her carefully in the Separation Doctrine, my friend had the unhappiness of actually seeing her come out of a cottage where she had been personally mixing with women of the lowest grade, and giving them things to eat."

"How very dreadful!"

"Yes. He confided the case to me. He said that he had passed over in silence her practice of going to church, because old habits linger. But this was too much for his patience. She had to be told in delicate but firm language that the engagement was broken off. The sequel showed that we were right."

" What was that ?"

" Instead of sorrowing over her failure to reach the Higher Level, this unhappy girl said that she was already tired of it, and shortly afterwards actually married a Clerical Fellow !"

" What a shocking thing !" said Miranda, deeply interested in this anecdote.

Paul Rondelet had been speaking with great solemnity, because all this was part of the Higher Level, and meant to prepare Miranda.

Now he began to speak more solemnly still.

" You have seen us, Miss Dalmeny," he went on. " At least you have seen me— one of our School. It has been my privilege to make your acquaintance in the Abbey of Thelema—a place, so to speak, of half culture. There are, that is, the elements of the Higher Culture, prevented from full development by such members as Caledon and others——"

" My very dear friends," said Miranda.

"Pardon me. I am speaking only from the—from my own point of view. No doubt, most worthy people. However, I have fancied, Miss Dalmeny, that in you I have seen the possibility of arriving at the Higher Level"—Miranda thought that this man was really the greatest of all Prigs she had ever seen. "In fact," he added, with a quiet smile, "one is never mistaken in these matters, and I am *sure* you are worthy of such elevation."

"Really, Mr. Rondelet, I ought to be very much gratified."

"Not at all; we learn discernment in the Higher Criticism. I saw those qualities in you from the beginning. But I have reflected, and, Miss Dalmeny, if you will accept me as your guide to the regions of the Higher Thought, we will together tread those levels, and make of life a grand, harmonious poem, of which not one word shall be intelligible to the Common Herd. Its very metre, its very rhythm, shall be unintelligible to them."

"If you please, Mr. Rondelet, leave the language of allegory, and tell me, in that of

the Common Herd, what it is you ask me
to do."

He turned red. After this magnificent
overture, leading to a short *aria* of extraordinary novelty, to be asked to clothe his
meaning in plain English—it was humi-
liating.

" I mean," he explained, after a gulp of
dissatisfaction, and dropping his eye-glass
once—" I mean, Miss Dalmeny, will you
marry me ?"

" Oh———h !" Miranda did not blush,
or tremble, or gasp, or faint, or manifest any
single sign of surprise or confusion. It was
as if she had been asked to go for a drive.
" You ask me if I will marry you. That is
a very important question to put, and I must
have a little time to answer it. No—do not
say any more at present. We shall meet
in the evening as if this talk had not been
held. Good-morning, Mr. Rondelet."

She rose in her queenly fashion, and
walked across the lawn to the house, leaving
him confused and uncertain.

Had she appreciated him ? Did she
realise what he brought to her ? He re-

flected with satisfaction that his method of approaching the subject had at least the merit of novelty.   Certainly, very few women had ever been invited to contemplate matrimony in such a manner.

CHAPTER VII.

"He's armed without who's innocent within."

THREE days before the wedding, Harry made
no sign and sent no message to Alma. But
she had faith. It *could* not be that a man
like her Harry, backed as he was by Mr.
Caledon, would fail her. She was perfectly
certain that all would be well, and she waited
in patience, no longer trying to please, and
careless about pretending to be a lady.

In fact, the conspirators were not idle.
Tom went to town, in order to obtain what
Desdemona called the most important of the
properties—the special license. The clergyman was found in an old friend of Tom's,
who consented, on learning the whole circumstances, to perform the ceremony. The

plot was, in fact, completely worked out, and, as Desdemona said, nothing remained but to hope that the situations would go off without any hitch.

On Wednesday, things being in this forward state, Desdemona and Tom walked across the park to the gamekeeper's cottage. It was empty, but the door stood open—a proof that the owner was not very far away— and the two entered the little room with its smoked and blackened rafters, which seemed dark after the blinding sunlight, and sat down to await Harry's return.

" This is like plunging into a cave to concert a robbery with a band of brigands," said Desdemona, taking Harry's wooden armchair. " In fact, I never felt so much like a conspirator before, not even on the stage. And as for the stage, the illusion is all in the front. . . . Tom," she resumed, after a pause, " I do not like it at all."

" Nor do I," Tom confessed.

" I can see you do not. ' How in the looks doth conscious guilt appear.' If it were only not for Lord Alwyne and Miranda——"

" It does seem hard," said Tom, " that a

fellow can't be allowed to make himself a fool in his own way."

" That is not the way to put it at all," said Desdemona, rousing herself for an apology. " Let me put it so that we shall be able to comfort ourselves with noble motives. All wicked people do that, you know. Fancy the pious rapture of Guy Fawkes just before he was going to light the match ; think of the approval which the conscience of Ravaillac must have bestowed upon him on the king's coach coming in sight. Let us apply the same balms to our own case. People may say—people who don't understand motives— that we two were Alan's most intimate and trusted friends, and that, notwithstanding, we deliberately conspired together to frustrate his most cherished project."

" I think, Desdemona," said Tom, " that you must have learned the art of comforting a sinner from the Book of Job. To be sure, people may say that ; but you forget that we haven't been found out yet. And Harry won't tell."

" It will come out some day," said Desdemona, gloomily. " Crimes like ours always do come out. I shall very likely reveal the secret on my death-bed. That will be a bad job for you. Or else you will go mad with the suspicion that I may some day tell, take me to a secret place in a forest, push me down a deep well, and drop big stones on my head. I shall creep out when you are gone, nothing the worse except for a bump as big as a cricket-ball on my skull, and a broken leg; and I shall creep after you, taking revenge in separate lumps as the opportunity offers. When I have got all the revenge that a Christian woman wants, I shall disclose myself, and you will die—under the lime-light, repentant, slowly, and to the music of the stringed instruments."

"Thank you," said Tom. "Now, tell me, please, how we ought to put it to ourselves."

"Thus," said the actress. "This extravagance of Alan affects others beside himself. The result of the step he proposes would be so disastrous that at any cost it must be prevented. He does not know the girl whom he is going to marry; he has conceived an entirely wrong impression of her character. His father, my old friend——"

" And mine," said Tom, feeling comfort in that reflection.

" Will be deeply grateful to us. Miranda will be grateful. After a time, Alan will be grateful; and as for the rest of the world, why—*il y a des reproches qui louent.*"

" Yes—and—Harry ? Do you think he will be grateful after a time, too ?" asked Tom. " You see, Desdemona, your estimate of the young lady's character is not a high one."

" Grateful ? Well, in a way. The man's in love with her. He does not, in his heart, believe that she is a bit better than the majority of women in her class. But just now it is good for him to think so. Depend upon it, Tom, it is not a bad thing for a man to find out that his wife is no better a human creature than himself, probably not so good."

" Desdemona," said Tom, "don't be hard on your sex."

" I am not," she replied ; " I am only just. Do you think Nelly an angel ?"

" Yes," he said stoutly, " I do, and I don't want any other kind of angel. People my paradise with one angel, and let her be Nelly, with all her moods and wilfulness, just as she is. I shall be satisfied."

"You are a good fellow, Tom, and you deserve her. Pity that, while you were about it, you could not have made that little document in your pocket a transferable ticket. We might then, at the very last moment, change the names from Harry and Alma to Tom and Nelly."

He shook his head sadly.

"The good old days!" she lamented. "Oh for a postchaise and four, and Gretna Green! or for a Fleet parson! What opportunities our ancestors had!"

"You can get a special license now," said Tom; "costs five guineas—that is what I've got for Harry."

"It is the one thing they have left us. Then, Tom, if you do not immediately—but here comes the third conspirator."

Tom explained to Harry that he had gone to London in order to obtain, through certain legal persons, a document which made it possible for him and Alma to get married to each other. And then he handed him the precious epistle.

"And with this bit o' paper," said Harry, doubtfully, "it is lawful for Alma and me to marry?"

He turned it all ways to catch the light, and blushed to think of the solicitude of the greatest persons in the realm after his welfare.

"And now," said Desdemona, "when shall we marry them?"

"The sooner the better," said Harry. "If there's going to be words, best have them over."

He was thinking of Bostock, but it seemed almost as if he was thinking of future matrimonial jars.

"We might manage on Friday," said Tom. "I am afraid it is too late to arrange for to-morrow. My friend the curate will do it on any day. After the marriage you can drive to Dalmeny Hall, and then send for Mr. Dunlop and have it out. You can tackle the Bailiff afterwards."

"Ay," said Harry; "I'm not afeard of the Bailiff. There'll be a vast of swearing, and that's all. Bailiff Bostock knows me. It is the Squire I am afeard on. He'll take it hard : me an old servant, and—there—once almost a friend I was, when we were both boys."

" You are a friend of his still, Harry," said Tom. " When he understands that it was your own bride he was going to take, it will all come right. But perhaps just at first there may be some sort of shindy."

" It cannot be on Friday," said Desdemona. " I remember now that Alma's wedding-dress is not to be ready till Friday afternoon. The poor girl must wear her fine frock, if only for once. You must arrange, Tom, to get the ceremony over and to drive back to the Hall before they ought to be starting for church. That, I think, will be the most effective as well as the most considerate way of leading up to the situation. It is not bad, as dramas go." She sprang from her chair, alert and active, and became again an actress. " A rehearsal. Stand there, Harry, as far back as the footlights—I mean the fender—will allow. Miranda and I are grouped here in an attitude of sympathetic expectation." (Here her face suddenly assumed a look of such deep sympathy, that Tom burst out laughing, and Harry was confounded.) " Alan is in the centre, up the stage; on your arm, Harry, is Alma." (Harry involuntarily glanced at his manly arm, as if Alma might really, by some magic of this wonderful lady, be there, but she was not.) " She is in her beautiful wedding frock and bonnet; she is looking shy and a little frightened, but so pretty that she has engaged the sympathies of the whole house. Alan, taken by surprise, moves a half-step forward; Miranda and I, surprised and wondering, take a half-step nearer him; we murmur our astonishment; Miranda, who is statuesque, and therefore does not gesticulate, turns her eyes mutely upon Alma; I, who am, or was thirty years ago, *mignonne*, hold up my hands—it is a very effective gesture, if done naturally; and then, Tom (I am afraid I *must* put you in the last scene, and concealment will be impossible), you step forward— oh, Tom !" (here she betrayed a little irritation because Tom, instead of throwing himself into the situation, was actually grinning), " why *can't* you act a little ? You step forward easily and quietly—you make a point, because your knowledge is the key of the whole situation—and you say, taking Alma by the hand, 'Alan, let me present to you—Harry Cardew's wife!' Now, that is really a very telling situation, if you could only think of it."

"I did not think of the situation," said Tom.

"No, you silly boy, you did not." Desdemona sat down again, and put off the actress. "If people would only think of the situation, and how it would look on the stage, none of the silly things, and only the picturesquely wicked things, would be done. 'All the world's a stage.' Yes; and there is always an audience. And none of us ever play our little part without some to applaud or some to hiss. They are a sympathetic audience, and they express their feelings vigorously. Dear me! he does not think of the situation. Live, Harry Cardew, as if you were always on the boards—walk, talk, think, as if you were speaking before the theatre. Do you understand?"

The honest gamekeeper did not. He had never seen a theatre.

"However," continued Desdemona, "we

are preparing the last scene of a comedy which will be numerously attended, and keenly criticised, so to speak; we must not spoil it by carelessness in the final tableau. We must make all we can out of it. As for you, Harry, you will be a hero for a few days. And you, Tom, must make up your mind to criticism. Play your part boldy. Make your mark in the last act. In the evening there will be a grand Function in the Abbey, at which you, too, ought to be a hero."

"And the row with Bostock?" asked Harry, who believed that this lady was able to control the future exactly; "has your ladyship fixed when and where that is to come off?"

"No; in fact, I quite forget that detail. But it does not matter so much, as it will not probably get into the papers. A mere piece of by-play, an episode. It ought, perhaps, to come before the last situation; but, after all, it does not greatly signify. I suppose the farmer is certain to use language of the strongest."

" After all—saving your ladyship's presence

—what," asked Harry, " what matters a few
damns ?"

" Nothing," said Desdemona, quoting Bob
Acres. " They have had their day. And
now, Harry, take great care of the document.
We shall tell Alma—not to-morrow, but on
Friday. Perhaps a hint to-morrow will keep
up her spirits.

" He is much too good for her," said Desdemona ; " but I am in hopes it will turn out
well. There is one great point in favour of
their happiness."

" What is that ?"

" She is afraid of him," said Desdemona,
student of womankind. " A wholesome terror
of her husband, with such a girl, goes a long
way. She will feel that she has got a man
to rule her."

At the Abbey they found that Lord Alwyne
had arrived. He was, in fact, sitting with
a bevy of Sisters. Nothing, he was wont to
say, more effectually removes the cares of the
world or makes a man forget his own age,
sooner than the society of young and beautiful ladies. He ought to have been born in

the seventeenth century, and basked in the gardens of Vaux, or beneath the smiles of the ladies who charmed away the declining years of La Fontaine. When Desdemona's tea was taken to her cell, Lord Alwyne came with it, and the fraternity, even including Miranda, abstained from entering that pleasant retreat, because they knew that the talk would be serious and would turn on Alan.

"I found myself growing anxious," Lord Alwyne said. "I hoped to learn that you had done something, that something had been done by somebody, somehow, to break it off. But the days passed by, and no letter came. And so—and so I have come down to learn the worst : of course, nothing can happen now to stop it." He looked wistfully at Desdemona. "It is too late now."

"Why, there are three whole days before us. This is Wednesday. What may not happen in three days ?"

"Desdemona, have you anything to tell me ?"

"Nothing, Lord Alwyne." She kept her eyes down, so that he should not read her secret there. " Nothing," she repeated.

" But there will be something ?"

"Who knows? There are yet three days, and at all events we may repeat what I said a month ago—they are not married yet."

" Then I may hope? Desdemona, have mercy."

She looked up, and saw on the face of her old friend a pained and anxious expression which she had never before seen. No man had ever spent a more uniformly happy, cheerful, and yet unselfish life. It seemed as if this spoiled son of fortune naturally attracted the friendship of those only who were fortunate in their destinies as well as in their dispositions. Misfortune never fell upon him or upon his friends. It gave Desdemona a shock to see that his face, as bright at fifty-five as at twenty-five, was capable of the unhappiness which has generally quite distorted the features of men at that age.

" My dear old friend," she cried, " what am I to say? I cannot bear to see you suffer. Have more than hope. Have confidence."

He took her hand and raised it to his lips with a courtesy more than Castilian.

"I ask no more, Desdemona. Tell me another time what you have done."

"You will have to thank Tom Caledon," she replied. "It is he, and a third person who is indispensable, whom you will have to thank."

"Tell me no more, Desdemona. What thanks of mine could equal this service? Tell me no more."

He was more deeply moved than Desdemona had ever seen him.

"I have been making myself wretched about the boy," he said, walking up and down the room. "It was bad enough to read of his doings with a pitchfork and a cart : it would make the most good-tempered man angry to be asked in the clubs about the Shepherd Squire, his son ; but that only hurt Alan himself. Far worse to think that he was going to commit the—the CRIME of marrying a dairymaid."

"I suppose," said Desdemona, "that it is natural for you to think most of the *mésalliance:* I dare say I should myself, if I had any ancestors. What I *have* thought of most is the terrible mistake of linking himself for life with such a girl, when he might have had —even Miranda perhaps. You cannot expect me quite to enter into your own point of view."

"I do not defend myself, Desdemona," said the man of a long line, with humility, as if he felt the inferiority of his position. "It is part of our nature, the pride of birth. Alan ought to have had it from both sides. I taught him, from the first, to be proud of the race from which he sprung. I used to show him the family tree, and talk to him about his predecessors, till I feared I was making him as proud of his descent as a Montmorenci or a Courtenay. In my own case, the result of such teaching was a determination to keep the stream as pure as I found it, or not to marry at all. With him the result is, that it does not matter how much mud he pours in, provided he can carry out an experiment. He fools away his children's pride for a hobby. To do this wrong to his children seems to me, I own, even a worse crime than to forget his ancestors."

"I see," said Desdemona, "what I call a misfortune you call a crime."

"Every misfortune springs from a crime, my dear Desdemona," said Lord Alwyne, sententiously. "This anxiety has made me feel ten years older; and when I thought I had lost my son I rejoiced, for the first time, to feel older."

"You will find him again, dear Lord Alwyne," she said softly, "in a few days. In fact, on Saturday. Remain with us till then. Perhaps it will be as well that you should not meet him, unless he hears that you have arrived. And reckon confidently on going home in ease of mind, and ready to commence again that pleasant life of yours which has no duties and no cares, but only friendships."

He took her hand again, and pressed it almost like a lover.

"Always the same, kind Desdemona," he said; "Clairette Fanshawe was the best woman, as well as the best and prettiest actress, that ever trod the stage. Do you think, Clairette"—it was twenty years since he had called her Clairette—"do you think that we really made the most of our youth while it lasted? Did we, *d'une main ménagère,* as the French poet advises, get the sweetness out of every moment? To be sure the memory of mine is very pleasant. I cannot have wasted very much of it."

" Perhaps," said Desdemona, smiling—she had spent the greater part of her youth in hard study, and the rest in bitter matrimonial trouble with a drunkard—" perhaps one lost a day here and there, particularly when there was work to do. It is unpardonable in a woman to waste her youth, because there is such a very little of it. But as for men, their youth seems to last as long as they please. You are young still, as you always have been. To be sure, your position was a singularly happy one."

"It was," said Lord Alwyne; "but you are wrong, Desdemona, in supposing that my life had no duties. My duty was to lead the idle life, so that it might seem desirable. Other people, hard-working people, learned to look upon it as the one for which they ought to train their sons. But it wants money; therefore, these hard-working people worked harder. Thus I helped to develop the national industry, and, therefore, the national prosperity. That is a very noble thing to reflect upon. Desdemona, I have been an example and a stimulus. And yet you say that I have had no duties."

CHAPTER VIII.

"Oh ! bid me leap, rather than marry Paris,
From off the battlements of yonder tower."

BROTHER PEREGRINE'S suit resembled, by
reason of its length, a suit in Chancery. It
never made any progress. He always carried
the same cheerful smile in his crowsfooted
eyes, always appeared in the same imperturb-
able good-humour. He never seemed to
notice whether the girl to whom he attached
himself was pleased to have him about her
or not, being one of those happy persons who
practised, though from a different motive, the
same cult of selfishness preached by Paul
Rondelet. He was a man who would play
with a child till it cried, when he would put
the plaything down and go away to find
another. His business was to amuse him-

self—"What is my land to one who is home from India, but a delightful garden full of pleasures?" The society of this beautiful and coquettish girl, full of odd moods and as changeable as a day in April, was pleasant to him—what did he care whether he was pleasant to her? He congratulated himself openly on his superiority to Tom, because he saw so much more of her.

But no progress. Plenty of compliments, pretty speeches without end; little presents of things from India, such as tiger-claw brooches, fans of scented wood, glass bottles gilded outside and filled with a tiny thread of precious essence, filigree work in silver, tiny chains of gold, bangles rudely worked—all these things accepted as part of his wooing. But the fatal words, which she feared and yet wished to have done with, so that there should be a final end with poor Tom—these did not come.

There was plenty of opportunity. Never was a place so admirably adapted for the interchange of such confidences as the Abbey of Thelema, with its corridors, cells, gardens, and wooded park. And at this juncture everybody seemed busily occupied in whispering secrets. What did the man mean? The situation, too, was becoming ridiculous; all the world—that is, the monastic world—watched it with interest. Also Mrs. Despard seemed, by her letters, to have some uneasy suspicion that all was not right. She even threatened to visit the Abbey herself, if only to expostulate, while yet there was time, with Alan Dunlop on his infatuated and suicidal intention. Most of her letters, in whole or in part, found their way to Tom—either they were read to him, or the contents were imparted to him in conversation.

"If she does come here, Tom," said Nelly, "which Heaven forbid, two things will happen immediately. You will have to leave the Abbey the day before her arrival, and—and—that other event will be settled at once."

"You mean——" said Tom.

"There is no occasion, Tom, to put everything into words."

Tom became silent.

"I think I have put too much into words already. I wonder," she went on, "whether you like me the better or the worse for telling you truthfully ?"

"Everything, Nelly," said Tom hoarsely, "makes me like you better every day."

"I *could* not, after your beautiful speech at the Court of Love, which went right to my heart, Tom—I *could* not bear you to think that I was only flirting with you all the time. I liked you too well. Poor Tom ! Do many other girls like you too ?"

"They don't tell me so if they do. But of course they don't. How girls ever do like men, I do not know."

"It is because they are not men," said the damsel wisely. " People would call it un-maidenly, I suppose, to tell a man—what I have told you—particularly when the man wants to marry you, and you can't marry him. But you don't think it unmaidenly, do you ?"

"As if you could do anything but what is sweet and good, Nell ! But you cannot know how much——"

"Hush, Tom ; don't put that into words— don't ; it only makes us both unhappy."

"Of course, I know," said Tom ruefully.

" I am next door to a pauper, and so are you, poor girl ; and we are both expensive people ; and there would be debts and things."

" Debts and borrowing, Tom, and not being able to pay back; and going on the Continent, and living in lodgings, and staying with people who would invite us, to save money. How should you like that ?"

" You always think of the worst, Nelly. There's Sponger, formerly of Ours, does that. Got two hundred a year ; goes everywhere, and is seen everywhere ; stays with people. They say he disappears for two months every year, when he is supposed to go to White-chapel and sweep a crossing where sailors are free with their coppers, I believe——"

Nelly interrupted this amusing anecdote.

" That is like you, Tom. Just as I was getting into a comfortable crying mood, when nothing does me so much good as a little sympathy, you spoil it all by one of your stupid stories. What do I care about Sponger of Ours ?"

" I thought you were talking about staying with people."

" Is the story about Sponger one of the

stories which the old novels used to tell us
kept the mess-room in a roar? If so, a mess-
room must be an extremely tiresome place."

This conversation took place on Wednesday afternoon. In the evening, to please
Lord Alwyne, Desdemona improvised a little
costume party, in which everybody appeared
in some Watteau-like dress, which was very
charming to the Sisters, and mightily became
such of the Monks as were well favoured.
They danced minuets and such things as
such shepherds and shepherdesses would
have loved. Brother Peregrine led out Nelly
for a performance of this stately old dance;
they went through it with great solemnity.

"Are they engaged?" asked Cecilia, watching them.

"I cannot tell, my dear," said Desdemona.
"The man is a riddle. Nelly does not look
at him the least as a girl generally looks on
an accepted lover. What does it mean?"

"I had a letter to-day," Cecilia went on,
"from Mrs. Despard. She says that Alan's
conduct has alarmed her so much that she
thinks of coming to take her daughter home.
I suppose she thinks that we are going to

follow Alan's example, and marry the dairyman's son, as he is engaged to the dairyman's
daughter.　It will be a great loss to us."

"Greater changes are going to happen,"
said Desdemona.　"Am I blind?　When do
you go, my child?"

Cecilia blushed prettily.　She was a very
charming girl, and her little idyl of love had
gone on quite smoothly, else I would have
told the story.　The commonplace lot is the
happiest; yet it does not read with much
interest.

"John——" she began.

"Brother Bayard," said Desdemona.　"I
shall always know him by that name."

"Wants to take me away at once; but I
shall insist on waiting till the autumn."

"May you be happy, my dear!

> "'You have consented to create again,
>   That Adam called 'the happiest of men.'"

Cecilia laughed.

"What you said the other night accelerated
things.　Desdemona, I should not be surprised if you were to receive a great many
confidences before long."

" And no jealousies among the Sisters ?"

" Not one.   We are all to be happy alike."

" That is as it should be," said Desdemona;
" and that is the true end of the Abbey of
Thelema."

" Only we are sorry for poor Tom, and for
Miranda, and for Alan.   We had hoped that
Miranda——"

"Alan is not married yet," said Desdemona.

Meantime, Nelly observed that her partner
was feverishly excited and nervous.   His
performance in the dance was far below his
usual form, and for the first time since she
had made his acquaintance he was not smiling.
That looked ominous.

" I have been," he whispered, in agitated
accents, when the dance was finished—" I
have been in the Garden of Eden for three
months, thanks to you.   Let me have a
quarter of an hour alone with you to-morrow.
Can it be that I am to take a farewell at the
gates of Paradise ?"

" I will meet you in the breakfast-room at
noon to-morrow," said Nelly quietly.

Farewell at the gates of Paradise ?   Was
the man really beginning to affect that self-

depreciation which to girls not in love seems
so absurd, and to girls who are in love is so
delightful ? He could not be in love as Tom
was—not in that fond, foolish way at least ;
there would be no sentiment, she said to herself, on either side. Then why begin with
nonsense about farewell ? Certainly there
would be no sentiment ; she would accept
him, of course, as she had told Tom all along.
It would be a bargain between them : he
would have a wife of whom Nelly was quite
certain he would be proud ; she would get as
good a house as she wanted, a husband *comme
il faut*, an establishment of the kind to which
she aspired in her most sensible moments,
and a husband who had his good points and
was amusing. It would have been better,
doubtless, to have a Tom Caledon, with
whom one could quarrel and make it up
again, whom one could trust altogether and
tell everything to, who would look after one
if there was any trouble. But, after all, a real
society husband, a life of society with people
of society, must be the best in the long-run.
Nelly felt that she should look well at her
own table and in her own drawing-room ; her

husband would talk cleverly; she would be tranquilly and completely happy. And as for Tom, why of course he would very soon forget her, and find somebody else—she hoped with money to keep him going. Poor Tom !

A life in the world against a human life; a sequence of colourless years against the sweet alternations of cloud and sunshine, mist and clear sky, which go with a marriage for love; a following of seasons, in which, year after year, social success grows to seem a less desirable thing, against the blessed recurrence of times sacred to all sorts of tender memories—was this the thing which Nelly had desired, and was going to accept, consciously?

I suppose it was her mother's teaching, whose book was

> "The eleventh commandment,
> Which says, ' Thou shalt not marry unless well.' "

That sweet womanly side of her character— the readiness to love and be loved—had been brought out by Tom, and yet it seemed, as an active force, powerless against the instructions of her childhood. It had been awakened by one brief erratic ramble into the realm of nature—that evening on Ryde pier—after which poor Nelly thought she had returned to the dominion of common sense. She hid nothing from Tom; she was as confiding as Virginia to Paul; but it did not occur to her that her decision, now that a decision was left to her, could possibly be other than that indicated by her mother.

She said that it was Fate. Just as the charity boy knows that it is perfectly useless as well as unchristian, to envy the Prince who rides past him on his own pony, so the girl, Nelly had learned, who has no *dot* may as well make up her mind at once that she cannot hope to follow the natural inclinations of her heart, and choose her own husband for herself. She must wait to be chosen, in this Babylonian marriage market, by the rich.

As for the other Sisters of the Abbey, they were all portioned, and could do as they pleased. Therefore Nelly looked with eyes of natural envy on this Sister, who could

listen to the suit of a penniless officer; and
on that, who, rich herself, was going to take
for better or for worse, and oh! how very
much for better, a love-sick youth richer than
herself. For them, the life of pleasantness,
the life of which we all dream, the life which
is not rendered sordid by money cares, and
mean by debts, and paltry in being bound
and cabined by the iron walls of necessity,
the life of ease had been attained. Men
work for it; giving it to wives and daughters
by early rising, late lying down, burning the
candle at both ends, and dying at fifty. Is
their lot worse than that of women who, to
obtain it, marry, and faithfully observe the
covenant of marriage with men whom, under
other circumstances, they would not have
preferred?

Nelly would have preferred Tom. There
was no doubt about that, none. But if she
could not marry Tom, being so very much
enamoured of the paths of pleasantness, why,
then, she must marry Mr. Exton; and he
seemed a cheerful creature, full of admiration
of her, and, doubtless, in his way, which was
very unlike the way of Tom, in love with her.

Perhaps as Nelly laid her fair head upon
the pillow that night her thoughts took up
some sad, defensive attitude.   But her pulse
beat no faster, and her sleep was not broken
by the thought of the morrow.

The pleasant breakfast-room, which looked
upon the inner court of the Abbey, was quite
deserted at noon, when Nelly arrived to
keep her appointment.   Mr. Exton did not
keep her waiting.

She sat down before a window, and waited,
with a little flush upon her cheek.

"How pretty you are!" sighed Brother
Peregrine.   His eyes were more curiously
crowsfooted than ever, and they had the
strangest look in them—a look the meaning
of which was difficult to make out.   Somehow, Nelly thought there was some sort of
shame in them, only Brother Peregrine was
surely the last person in the world to manifest that sort of emotion.   Besides, what was
there to be ashamed of ?   " I think that you
are growing prettier every day."   His face,
covered with its multitudinous crows'-feet,
seemed forced into a smile ; but there was no

mirth in his eyes. He had said much the
same sort of thing a good many times before,
but had never got beyond that kind of general
statement.

"Do you think it altogether right," asked
Nelly, looking him straight in the face, "to
say that sort of thing?"

"But that wasn't what I wanted to say,"
said the Brother, with considerable hesitation. "I—I—I am going to leave the
Abbey to-day. I have just written a letter
of farewell to the Order, and sent it to Desdemona——"

"Going to leave the Abbey, and why?"

"Because I must," he replied gloomily.
"Because, although these limbs seem free, I
wear the chains of slavery. Because I am
called away."

This was a very mysterious beginning.

"You talk as if you were going to the end
of the world."

"I wish I were. But I am only going to
London."

"Is that such a very dreadful place? To
be sure, at this time of year, there will be
nobody to talk to."

"I have had—the—the most DELIGHTFUL time," Brother Peregrine went on nervously; "and entirely through you. I shall never, certainly never, forget the walks, and drives, and talks you have given me. They have left the most charming recollection in my mind. I do not believe there is a sweeter girl than yourself in all the world—alas!"

He heaved the most melancholy sigh.

What *could* he mean? Leave recollections in his mind? Then, after all, he was not, perhaps, going to—— Nelly sat quite silent. Her cheeks had grown pale suddenly, and in her head were a dozen thoughts battling to take shape in her brain.

"Will you remember me, with a little regret?" he asked. "To be sure I cannot ask for more—a man in my awful position ought not to ask for so much——"

"When you explain yourself," said Nelly; "when I understand what your awful position is, I shall be better able to talk to you."

"I have told you I am sent for."

"Who has sent for you?"

"My wife," he replied simply.

His wife!

" She has just arrived from India, with all the children. She is at the Langham Hotel. She writes to me that unless I go to her at once she will come to me."

Nelly gazed at him with eyes of wonder. The man was shaking and trembling.

" You don't quite understand what that means," he went on. " Perhaps when I tell you that my wife is a—a—Eurasian, in fact, with more of the tar than of the lily in her complexion, and that the children take after their mother in complexion and temper, you may begin to understand that I was not particularly anxious to talk about my marriage."

" And so you pretended to be an unmarried man," said Nelly, a little bitterly.

" No one ever asked me if I was married," he said. " If they had, I dare say I should have confessed. She is much older than myself, and she has a temper. She is also jealous. Very jealous she is. The children have tempers too, and have been spoiled by their mother. They are not pleasant children at all."

" Was this all you had to say to me ?"

Nelly rose and stood at the window.

" Yes, I think so. Just to thank you for

your kindness, and to express a hope that you will not forget this summer."

"No, I am not likely to forget this summer," she replied, with a touch of bitterness in her tone; "not at all likely. Nor shall I readily forget you, Mr. Exton."

"Your advocate in the great case of Lancelot *versus* Rosalind," he said. "You will remember me by that, you know."

"I shall remember you," she said, "without thinking of the *Cour d'Amour*. And now, good-bye."

She held out her hand coldly. He bent over it, and would have kissed it, but she drew it back.

"No, Mr. Exton. Think of your wife. By the way, you are going to London? Mamma is, I believe, in town for a few days. Will you call upon her? She would like to make Mrs. Exton's acquaintance, I am sure. She might tell Mrs. Exton, too, more than you would be likely to remember about the Abbey of Thelema. Mamma's address is No. 81, Chester Square. You will be sure to call, will you not? Good-bye. I am sorry to hear that you are——"

" Married ?" he asked.

" No, not at all. . . . I am glad to hear that your wife has arrived. Husband and wife ought to be together. I am only sorry that we shall lose you. I can write to mamma, then, that you will call upon her to-morrow. It is No. 81, Chester Square. Do not forget. Good-bye, Mr. Exton."

With these words, the sting of which he hardly comprehended, but which, as Nelly intended, he would discover when that call was actually made, she left him, and, without looking to right or left, mounted the stairs and sought the privacy of her own cell.

There she sat down, and, with pale cheek and hardened eyes, tried to understand the position of things. She was bitterly humiliated; she was ashamed; angry with her mother, angry with herself, fiercely angry with the man who had played with and deceived her. How could she face the Sisters, all of them happy in the possession of a suitor about whom there was no mystery and no deception? Should she tell the whole story to everybody? Would it not be better to go on and make no sign? But some one she must tell. Desdemona would hear her story with sympathy; so would Miranda; so would . . . . and here there came a knock at her door. It was no other than Tom Caledon.

"Your reception-morning, Nell," he said awkwardly. "I come as a simple caller. But what is it, Nelly? You look pale. Has that fellow Exton——has he——"

"He has said good-bye to me, Tom."

"What? You have refused him, then? Oh! Nell, tell me."

"No, Tom, it is worse than that. I went prepared to accept him . . . and he did not . . . make the offer I expected. He is gone, Tom."

"Has the fellow been playing all the time then?"

"Not quite. I think he has been enjoying himself in his own way, without thinking how he might compromise me. But he is a married man, Tom. That is all. A married man. And his wife has ordered him home."

"A married man?"

"He says so. About such a trifle"—she laughed bitterly—"men do not generally tell lies, I suppose. He spoke very prettily about my kindness; and so I asked him, out of pure gratitude, Tom, to go to Chester Square and call upon mamma."

Tom stared blankly.

" Then he has imposed upon all of us."

" That does not matter, Tom.   I am the only person to be pitied—or blamed.   I, who have been allowed to stay down here on the condition that I was to—to throw myself in his way, to attract him, to please him, to court him, if necessary.   I, who was to pose before him like a dancing girl, to listen to his idle talk, always to be pleasant to him.   Oh! it is shameful—it is shameful!"

She stamped her little foot and wrung her hands, and the tears came into her eyes.

" I never thought before what it was like— this angling for rich men.   What must they think of us ?   What can you think of me, Tom ?"

" You know very well what I think of you, Nelly."

" Now I must go back to town, and it will all begin over again, as soon as mamma has found some one else.   Go away, Tom ; don't think of me any more.   I am only an adven-

turess. I am unworthy that you should be
kind to me. I shall leave this sweet place,
with all the Brothers and Sisters, and dear
Miranda and Desdemona—oh! the beautiful
home of rest—and go back again to the
world, and fight among other adventuresses."

" No, Nelly, no," cried Tom. And while
she sank her head into her hands his arms
were round her. " No, Nelly darling. I will
not let you. Stay here; stay with me, and
we will take our chance. Never mind the
world, Nell; we will give up the things that
only rich people can do. Stay with me, my
darling."

" Oh! Tom—Tom—will you take me?
And now?—you ought to have more self-
respect, Tom: now—after all that is passed?"

" This is real happiness, Tom," she said,
looking up in his face, with her full, deep
eyes. " There can be no happiness like this."

And so passed half-an-hour.

Then Nelly said that they must come back
to the world, and that meant punishing Mr.
Exton, in the first place.

" As I have sent him to call upon mamma,"

she said, "I must prepare mamma's mind for his visit."

She wrote the shortest of letters.

"DEAR MAMMA,

"Mr. Exton will call upon you to-morrow. I hope you will be at home.

"Your affectionate daughter,

"ELEANOR."

"There, Tom!" she said, with a mischievous light in her eye. "You see, that commits me to nothing, and it will lead mamma to think a great deal. The explosion, when she finds out, will be like a torpedo. I really think that I have punished poor Brother Peregrine enough."

This business despatched, Tom began upon another.

"Nelly," he said, "will you do exactly what I ask you?"

"Exactly, Tom," she said.

"No one, not even Desdemona, is to know it."

"No one, Tom."

Then he whispered in her ear for a few

minutes.   First she stared at him with all her eyes ; then she blushed ; then she laughed ; and then she trembled.

"Oh ! Tom, it is delightful.   But what *will* mamma say ?"

CHAPTER IX.

"Can these things be? or are visions about?"

IT was on Thursday afternoon that Miranda asked Mr. Rondelet to meet her in Desdemona's cell.

He came with a curious sense of agitation. It was hardly possible that she should refuse him ; and yet—why had she not accepted him at once ? What need to deliberate for four and twenty hours over what might just as well have been decided on the spot ? Perhaps, however, it was the way of young ladies, a class with whom Paul Rondelet, in spite of his monastic vows, had but little sympathy.

Had he overheard the conversation which took place between Desdemona and Miranda, he would have been more agitated.

"No," Miranda was saying. "You need not be in the least alarmed, Desdemona, I am not going to hold out any hopes. And this, I trust"—she heaved a deep sigh—"will be the last of my courtiers."

Desdemona lifted her great soft eyes lazily: she was lying, as usual, in her comfortable *chaise longue*, with a few costume designs in her lap, and laughed noiselessly.

"I should have dismissed him on the spot," Miranda went on, "but his condescension and conceit were so amazing that they irritated me. It is an ignoble thing to confess, but I longed to box his ears."

"My dear Miranda," said Desdemona, "I sincerely wish you had. Most young men, and especially young men of Advanced Thought, would be all the better for a box on the ears."

And just then the candidate for her hand and fortune appeared.

He was elaborately got up: a studied simplicity reigned in his neat and faultless dress, his grey kid gloves, the hat which was not too new and yet not shabby, the plain black silk ribbon which did duty for a tie.

Even his smooth cheeks, his tiny moustache, his dark hair parted down the middle with an ambrosial curl, half an inch long over his white brow, spoke of quintessential taste.

"Pray sit down, Mr. Rondelet," said Desdemona the hostess. "Take the chair nearest the china. I know it soothes you to be near blue china. Miranda has asked me to be present, if you do not object."

"Miss Dalmeny's wishes are commands," he said, feeling more uneasy. But perhaps she was going to take him at his word and enter upon a betrothal with the calm which marks the truly philosophic spirit. After all she *would* be worthy of him.

"I have been thinking, Mr. Rondelet," said Miranda slowly, turning a paper-knife between her fingers, and looking at her suitor with more of a critical eye than he liked to see. It is all very well to be a critic, but no critic likes to be criticised. She was looking, too, calm and self-possessed, as if she was perfectly mistress of the situation. "I have been thinking over what you said. You assumed, you may remember, as a ground for your request, a superiority over

the ordinary run of educated men—over our
Monks of Thelema, for instance. But I have
reflected, however, that I was asked to take
that on your own assurance. Would you
mind telling me how you can prove this
superiority?"

Proof? Proof of his superiority? Paul
Rondelet dropped his eye-glass and drew a
long breath of amazement. Then he put it
up again, and flushed a rosy red. Did she
actually want him to bring testimonials, like
a candidate for a place?

"I am Paul Rondelet," he said proudly—
"Paul Rondelet of Lothian. I should have
thought that was enough."

"We live here," said Miranda, "so far
from Oxford, and are so little connected with
the circles where people think, that I am
afraid I must ask you for a little more infor-
mation." Her voice was steady and her
manner calm, but in her eyes there was a
light which boded ill for her suitor. "I have
no doubt at all that you are incontestably in
the front. Only I should like to know how
you got there."

Paul Rondelet was silent. This was an

awkward turn of things. What reply could he make?

"For instance," Miranda went on pitilessly, "have you written works of scholarship?"

"No," said Paul, very red and uneasy, "I leave grammar to schoolmasters."

"Then there is Art," she continued. "The women of your higher levels, you say, are to possess an instinctive love for Art, but are to be trained by the men. Do you paint?"

Paul Rondelet, whose lips were very dry by this time, and his hands trembling, shook his head. He did not paint.

"Then how could you train me, supposing I possessed this instinct?"

"I should instruct you on the principles of Art and its highest expression," said the superior youth.

"Yes—yes. You would show me beautiful pictures. But I have already, we will suppose, the instinct of Art, and could find them out for myself. And all that you could tell me I have in my library already."

"The new school, the Higher School," he

interrupted pleadingly, "requires its own language to express its new teaching."

"I know," she said, "I have translated some of the language of the New School into English, and I find its disciples to be on no higher a level, as I think, than my old authorities. I have Ruskin, at least, whom I can understand. And Eastlake, and Wornum, and Jameson, and old Sir Joshua. However, there are other things. You have written novels, perhaps?"

He shuddered. Could a man of his standing condescend to write a novel, to pander to the taste of the vulgar herd who read such things?

"You are a dramatist, then?"

"The British Drama is dead," he replied in a hollow voice.

"Perhaps it is only sleeping. Perhaps some day a man will awaken it," she said. "But there is poetry; we know that you write verses. Are you a poet acknowledged by the world?"

This was dreadful. He had published nothing. And yet there were those little poems, which his friends carried in their bosoms, over which he had spent so many hours. But most certainly he could not show these to a lady so little advanced in the principles of his school.

"Then, Mr. Rondelet," said Miranda, "I am at a loss to know on what grounds your claims for superiority rest."

This was a decisive question. It demanded decision. But Rondelet rose from the chair in which he had endured this cross-examination with as much dignity as he could assume. Standing gives a speaker a certain advantage.

"I will endeavour to explain," he said.

"Oh! Miranda," cooed Desdemona in the softest and most sympathetic of murmurs, "Mr. Rondelet will explain. Oh yes; one always declared that he was a really superior man. One felt that if you wanted to know anything, you only had to ask him. How charming of him to explain!"

But Paul Rondelet thought he detected the faintest possible sarcasm in her accents, and he hated Desdemona for the moment with a hate inextinguishable.

"You have placed me, doubtless unintentionally, in an exceedingly difficult position," he said, with an artificial smile. "Such a superiority as you imagine, Miss Dalmeny I did not claim. You misunderstood me."

"Oh! Miranda," purred Desdemona. "You misunderstood him."

"What I meant was this," he said. "I belong to the school which possesses the Higher Criticism."

"Oh!" said Desdemona, clasping her hands.

Paul Rondelet began to hate this woman worse than ever.

"Our standard of Art is different from, and far above, that recognised by the world; we have our own canons; we write for each other in our own language; we speak for each other. It is not our business to produce, but if we do produce, it is after many years of thought, and whether it is only a small essay, or a single sheaf of sonnets, it is a production which marks an epoch in the development of Art."

"Are there many of these productions yet before the world?" pursued Miranda.

" As yet none. Some are carried about by ourselves for our own delight."

Miranda put down her paper-knife. Her face was quite hard and stern.

" You are a critic. Really, Mr. Rondelet, I never before heard so singular a proposal. You offer me, in return for my hand, to impart to me — the Higher Criticism."

Looked at in this cold, passionless way, the proposal did not indeed appear attractive even to the proposer.

" What else can you give me, Mr. Rondelet, beside the cold air of the Higher Levels ? Do you love me ?"

She asked this question in a business-like manner, which was at the same time most irritating. Never before in all his life had Paul Rondelet felt himself ridiculous.

" I thought," he said, " that you were superior to the vulgar . . . . . the vulgar . . . . ."

Here Miranda interrupted him.

" The vulgar desire of being loved by my husband ? Not at all, Mr. Rondelet, I assure you. I should, on the other hand, expect it."

" In the common sense of the word," he went on stammering. " I suppose—— But it is impossible for a man of my school to affect more than the esteem which one culti- vated mind feels for another."

" I am glad you have told me the exact truth," she said. " One likes to find respect for the truth even on your height. But tell me more, Mr. Rondelet. Do you wish to marry me only because you esteem me, or is there any other motive ?"

He hesitated, dropped his eye-glass, blushed, and lost his head altogether. At this mo- ment, standing limp and shattered before his interrogator, Paul Rondelet of Lothian looked like a guilty schoolboy.

" Are you rich, Mr. Rondelet ?"

" I—I—I am not," he replied.

" You have your Fellowship, I believe. Is that all ?"

" That is all," said Paul Rondelet.

He felt more limp, more like a guilty schoolboy, as he answered these questions.

" And when that ceases, you will have

nothing. I heard from Alan that it would cease in a few months."

" Yes," said Paul Rondelet.

" And after ?"

" I do not know."

" Do you think it worthy of a member of your school to look on marriage as a means of maintaining himself in ease ?"

" It is not that," he replied eagerly—" not that—I mean—not—altogether that. It is true that—in fact—any man might look forward to—to——"

" Come, Mr. Rondelet," said Miranda, " I am sure this conversation is painful to you. Let us stop. As for my answer, you may readily guess it."

He hung his head, and tried in vain to put up his eye-glass.

" Let us be friends, Mr. Rondelet," she went on, holding out her hand.

He took it feebly.

" You will yet show the world that you have ability apart from the—the Higher Criticism, I am sure. Besides, a leader ought to teach."

" That is not our creed," murmured Paul

Rondelet, trying to reassert himself; "we live our own life to ourselves. Let others see it and imitate us if they can."

" But how, with no income, will you live the life? Can criticism, even of the highest, provide you with what you have taught yourself to consider necessaries? Must you not think how you will live any life at all?"

" I do not know," groaned the unfortunate man.

" Will you write for the papers?"

He shuddered.

" Am I to give *my* thoughts to the vulgar herd to read over their breakfast?"

It was no use being angry with the man. His conceit was sublime. But Miranda spoke with impatience.

" There is no common herd. We are all men and women together. Believe me, Mr. Rondelet, you have lived too long in Oxford. The air of Lothian College is unwholesome. Go out of it at once, and fight among the rest, and do your little to help the world along. God knows we want all the help we can get."

He only stared in a helpless way.

"Your level?" she asked, with a little laugh. "You will find it where you find your strength. Perhaps, some day, when other people are ready to place you above them, you will be ashamed of ever thinking yourself on a higher level than the rest. Your school? That is a paltry and a selfish school which begins with scorn for the ignorant. The common herd?"—she stamped her foot with impatience—"why, we are all one common herd together : some richer, some poorer, and some a little stronger. And there is only one hope for the world, that men and women help each other, as Alan Dunlop has set himself to help his people."

The tears came into her eyes for a moment, but she brushed them away, and made a gesture of dismissal. The crushed Fellow of Lothian obeyed the gesture, and without a word withdrew.

Miranda remained where she stood for a few moments, silent, tearful.

"I compared him with Alan," she said. "Oh ! the *little* creature that he showed beside our glorious Alan !"

"You are a queen, Miranda," said Desdemona, "and Alan is——"

"What is Alan?" she asked, with a little laugh.

"He is Hamlet, Prince of Denmark."

CHAPTER X.

"Sinful brother, part in peace."

On that Thursday evening, when Refectory bell rang, it was discovered that no fewer than four of the Brothers were absent, an event remarkable in the chronicles of the Abbey.

Alan Dunlop, who, during this week, his last of celibacy, naturally devoted his evenings entirely to his bride, was one. His father was present, however—no unworthy substitute. Tom Caledon was absent too. Where was Tom?

Everybody quite naturally looked to Nelly.

" Tom has gone to town on business," said Nelly quietly.

13—2

Then, without any apparent reason, she blushed deeply, so that the monastic fraternity smiled.

Mr. Paul Rondelet was absent. The reason of this was that he was perfecting a grand scheme which he proposed to lay before Alan immediately. Also, his interest in the Abbey had greatly diminished since Miranda's few plain words.

And where was Brother Peregrine—the man who had been so useful in keeping things going, who had been everywhere at once, and was Desdemona's right-hand man for invention, as Tom Caledon had been for execution? Where was Brother Peregrine, who had been for three months the devoted follower of Nelly? Had she refused him?

"After dinner," said Desdemona, "I will tell you what has become of Brother Peregrine."

"I have," she said, when the inner man had been refreshed, and there was nothing on the table but claret and fruit—"I have to read a very sad letter. The Order of Thelema has been imposed upon. You will all be sorry to learn that Brother Peregrine has traded upon our credulity, and intruded himself upon us under false pretences."

There was considerable sensation. Desdemona, with the deliberation acquired on the stage, proceeded slowly to unfold a letter and lay it open. You know how they do it : a quick movement of the hand breaks the seal; a look up to the first circle expresses expectation, terror, or joy; the letter is torn from the envelope ; that is thrown to the ground ; both hands are used to unfold it, and one smooths it out. Then, with another glance, but at the pit this time, the letter is brought to the focus of the eye, and read slowly.

That is the stage method. Desdemona could not help adopting it under the present circumstances. She read it with a running commentary :

"'Dear Sister Desdemona'—he has the audacity to call me sister after what has happened!—'For the last time, before laying aside the monastic garb, which I never ought to have assumed, I venture to address you by a title under which you will always be remembered by me'—I dare say he will remember all of us by our monastic names—the wretch!—' I am not, I confess with shame, legally entitled to the status and position under the pretence of which I took your vows. By the statutes, the Abbey receives none but the unmarried '"—here there was a general movement of surprise—"' except in your own case '—and I am a widow," said Desdemona. —"' Such an exception I knew could not be made in my own case; it would have been idle to ask or to expect it. And yet the truth was, and is, that I have the misfortune of being a married man.'"

There was a profound sensation. One or two laughed—they were of the masculine order. The Sisters looked indignant. Cecilia said it was shameful, and asked what punishment could be inflicted on such a monk.

"He is not only a false pretender," she cried, "but he is unfaithful to his vows, because he derides the state of matrimony."

Then Nelly's sweet voice was lifted up, and everybody felt that she had a special right to be heard.

"Yes," she said, "it is quite true. He told me so himself this morning. You all thought

he was paying his addresses to me. So did
I. So did Tom. It made him jealous."

"Yes," said Miranda, "we all know that.
But can we punish him, and how ?"

"I have punished him already," said
Nelly.

She blushed and kept her eyes on her
plate.

"I think you will all understand when I tell
you that I have made him promise to call
upon mamma," she murmured. "He will call
to-morrow morning."

They looked at one another and smiled.
Everybody at once concluded that things
would be made unpleasant for this sinful
Brother. Then Desdemona went on reading
the letter :

"'I have the misfortune of being a married
man. My wife and children, whom I left in
India, her native country, have now arrived,
and are at the Langham Hotel. She has
found out my address, most unfortunately,
and writes me word that unless I return to
London instantly, she will come down here.
To spare the Order a visit from that lady, I

am on the point of returning to town without loss of time.

" ' Will you kindly assure the Fraternity that, while I feel that nothing can possibly excuse my conduct, I shall always rejoice in a deception which enabled me to enjoy three most delightful months ?   The Sisters are more charming than, with my unfortunate experience, seemed possible for ladies ; wedlock under such circumstances would not, I feel convinced—— but I have no right to speak of such things.   If they are disposed to be angry with me, they may perhaps reflect upon my situation, and accord me their pity.

" ' I bid farewell to the Abbey with the deepest regret.   As my wife proposes to remain in England for the education of her children, I shall return to India immediately. Indeed, I have already taken steps, by means of the Submarine Telegraph Company, to ensure the reception of an urgent message calling me back by the next boat, to look after my estates.   I shall therefore reside in Assam until my family shall have completed their education, and, with their mother, return to

India. I hope, then, to get back to England. I may explain, if anybody is curious about my history, that the plantation is very large and lucrative, and that it was originally her own.

" ' Your sorrowful and afflicted Brother,

" ' Peregrine.' "

A Resolution was passed that Brother Peregrine's name should be without further delay erased from the list of the Fraternity : and that he should no more be mentioned in any of their Functions or Rejoicings. But there was some sympathy expressed, and, perhaps, had the Brother pleaded his own defence in person, he might have obtained forgiveness.

But there would be few more Functions. The end of the Abbey—of this particular branch of the Order of Thelema—was rapidly approaching, though no one realised it except Desdemona.

In all the histories of human communities which I have read, this of the Abbey of Thelema is the only one in which petty jealousies, ambitions, and desire to rule have found no place. Miranda was absolute

Queen, Desdemona was Prime Minister, or
First Vizier; she was also Directress of
Ceremonies. Alan, by universal consent,
acted as Orator, while Brother Bayard, the
stately, was with equal unanimity appointed
Herald, whenever a splendid person of that
description was required. There were no
committees, no governing bodies, no elec-
tions, nothing to raise ambitious hopes or
revolutionary designs. It would be worth
the while of Club Committees to imitate the
constitution of the Abbey. There must be
some clubs where more is thought of the
candidate himself than of his subscription.
In the Abbey of Thelema were none of those
who disturb and vex club life—among those
who talked were neither down-criers, nor
slanderers, nor stabbers in the back; none
were jealous one of the other—none were
anxious that his neighbour should fail—there
were no petty ambitions—there was no talk
of money or desire of κῦδος. Could we
get such a club in London—could we keep
it in its original purity—could we ensure
the retirement of a discordant member—we
should call into existence the means of

making the most despondent of philosophers find joy in life.

"It is a delightful place, Desdemona," said Lord Alwyne; "but, unless an experienced eye is wrong, there will shortly be many changes. They go when they marry, do they not, your Brothers and Sisters?"

"Alas! yes," sighed Desdemona. "The Monastic vows do not contemplate continued residence. And the wedding ring takes a Sister into the outer world."

CHAPTER XI.

"Hic est aut nusquam quod quærimus."

MR. PAUL RONDELET was refused, with a plainness of speech which left no room for doubt. He was indignant, he was humiliated ; but it was absurd to suppose that the ignorance of a girl was to make him disbelieve in himself. Not at all. What he was before Miranda treated him with such unworthy estimate, such he was still. Was he, Paul Rondelet of Lothian, to be cast down because Miss Dalmeny, a mere country girl, did not know who and what he was ? Certainly not ; he was saddened, naturally. Perhaps he had thought that his reputation extended even to so low a stratum of culture as that of the Abbey; perhaps he had hoped that the name of Rondelet was known in wider circles. It was a pity, a grievous pity, he thought. He might have made a charming home, on the newest principles, of Dalmeny Hall; he was eminently a man to grace, as it had never before been graced, the position of country squire; and that might have been his position had Miranda taken him on his own estimate, without wanting to measure him by the ordinary standards of what he had done. What he had done, indeed! What he had thought, would have been the proper question. But until Research is endowed, he felt, with sadness, men like himself have no proper chance.

Meantime, he set to work with vigour to elaborate an idea which was at once to ensure his immortality and to prove his greatness. No doubt there was a touch of *rancune*, a desire to show Miranda what kind of man she had contemptuously refused. He dined in his own cell, read over his scheme by the rosy light of a bottle of Château Laffitte, gave it the finishing touches, and at nine o'clock sallied forth, manuscript in pocket, in search of Alan Dunlop.

His idea was based, financially speaking,

on the grand fact that Alan was rich.   Rich
men are needful for the help of those who
are poor.   To submit an idea to a rich man,
provided he be capable of receiving an idea,
is to do him the great service of making him
use his wealth.   Alan was eminently recep-
tive of ideas.   And Paul Rondelet marvelled
that he had neglected to *exploiter* this wealthy
mine during so many years.   His own disciple, almost—his admirer, always—one who
believed in him—it was absurd to think of
going out into poverty with Alan at his back.

He made his way to the Shepherd Squire's
comfortless cottage, and waited there for his
arrival.

Nothing was changed in the cottage since
that first day when Alan went to sleep by the
fire, and awoke to find his breakfast stolen.
There was the wooden chair beside the deal
table ; the shelf of books ; the stack of papers,
the cupboard door open, showing the common
china and the materials for making tea, bread
and butter, and other simple accessories of a
hermit's life.   The kettle was on the hob,
though the fire was not lit ; and a couple of
candlesticks stood upon the mantel-shelf.

Paul Rondelet lit the candles, sat, and waited. This cottage life, he remembered, was one of the dreams of a certain stage in his own development. He thought how, in their ardent youth, they had taken their claret in Alan's rooms, which looked over the stately college gardens, and discussed the life of self-sacrifice which was to regenerate the world. There were a dozen who formed their little set of theorists. Out of them all one alone was found to carry theories into practice, and realise a dream. What about himself? What about the rest? It was not enough to say that they were men who had to make an income for themselves. He could no longer comprehend the attitude of mind which made such a dream as that former one possible. He had grown out of it, he said. He had sunk beneath it, conscience whispered; but then the Advanced School does not believe in conscience. And the rest? They were all at work: practising at the Bar, writing, teaching, even—melancholy thought!—curates and parish priests.

What he could no longer understand was the nobleness of the nature which thus simply converted theory into practice, and became what the others only talked about. What he failed to see was, that, living in slothful ease, which he mistook for intellectual activity, he had lost the power to conceive any more, far less to execute, the noble dreams of his youth.

He sat and wondered. Six years before, his heart would·have burned within him, and his spirit would have mounted upwards, to join that of Alan Dunlop. Now he only wondered.

Presently Alan came. His manner was listless, his face was haggard. Alma had been more than usually unreceptive that evening. She had been sulky; she had returned rude and short answers; she had tried his patience almost beyond his strength. His father too, he had learned, was at the Abbey, and he did not dare go to see him, lest in his tell-tale face, or by his tell-tale tongue, it should be discovered that he had made a great and terrible mistake, beyond the power of an honourable man to alter.

" You here, Rondelet ?"

"Yes, I have been waiting for you. Let us have a talk, Alan."

Paul Rondelet produced his roll of papers, while Alan, with rather a weary sigh, took down a pipe from the mantel-shelf, filled it, and sat listlessly on his deal table.

" Go on, Rondelet ; I am listening."

Paul Rondelet began, with a little nervousness unusual to him, to expound his project. Had Alan cared to read between the lines, his speech would have been as follows :

" I am driven to the necessity of doing something for myself ; in a few months I shall have no income. I can find no way of fighting as men generally do fight. I can discern no likely popularity in what will fall from my pen. I want to get, somehow or other, endowment. You are a very rich man. You shall endow me."

What he really said at the finish was this :

" I will leave the Prospectus with you. I shall be able to find a publisher—on commission—easily. It is a crying shame that a magazine purely devoted to the followers of the Higher Culture does not exist."

" There are the *Contemporary*, the *Fortnightly*, the *Nineteenth Century*."

" My dear Dunlop !"—he held up his hands

—" pray do not think that we are going to occupy *that* level.   We shall have none but our own circle as readers, writers, and supporters."

" Will you depend on names ?"

" On some names, yes.   Not on the names of ex-Premiers; only on the names of those who are men of mark among ourselves."

" But—do you think it will pay ?"

" Not at first, I suppose—eventually.   And that brings me to my next point.   I have drawn up a note of expenses.   I put myself down as editor, with eight hundred pounds a year.   You do not think that excessive, Dunlop ?"

" Surely not, for a man of your calibre."

" The rest of the estimate you can go into at your leisure.   I want you, as the most advanced of our wealthy men, to guarantee— to guarantee," he repeated, with an anxious flush of his cheek, " not to give, the expenses of the first year.   Whatever loss there may be, if any, will be repaid from the subsequent profits."

Alan received this proposition in silence. Only he stroked his beard and pulled at his pipe. His domestic experiments had already cost him so much that he was loath to incur fresh responsibilities.

" To guarantee, not to give," repeated Paul Rondelet, glancing at his face uneasily. "Consider," he went on. "We, who set an example in our lives, should also set an example in our writings. It is not preaching that we want, but the acted life." That was just what Alan, in a different way, had always maintained. " Let the lower herd, the crowd, see how we live, read what we write, and learn what we think."

" Y-yes," said Alan doubtfully ; "and the probable amount of the guarantee—what one might be asked to pay, month by month ?"

" That," said Mr. Rondelet airily, " is impossible for me to say. Perhaps a thousand in the course of the year. Perhaps a little more. We shall have, of course, a great quantity of advertisements to fall back upon. I have no doubt that we shall rapidly acquire a circulation. People want guidance : **we** shall guide them : they want to know what to think—we shall formulate their thoughts :

14—2

what to read—we shall publish a list of selected articles."

" That sounds possible," said Alan, softening.

"You and I, my dear Alan," went on the tempter, "will be registered joint proprietors. You shall find the money : I will find the staff. You shall start us : I will be the editor. And we will share the profits."

"Yes. I was to share the profits of my farm ; but there are none."

" There will be, in this magazine. Fancy a monthly journal without a trace of Philistinism in it. Positively no habitant of the Low Country allowed to write in it. The Higher Thought demands a style of its own. There have been articles, I own, in the *Fortnightly*, especially written by members of our own school, which none but ourselves could possibly understand. Picture to yourself a paper absolutely unintelligible save to the disciples of the New School. As for the other things, what can be expected from magazines which allow Bishops, Deans, Professors, and people of that sort to contribute ?"

Paul Rondelet shook his head sadly, as if

the lowest depth must be reached when you come to Bishops. Alan was shaken, but not convinced. Sitting as he was among the ruins of his own schemes, he was naturally not anxious to promote new ones. And yet, the old influence of Paul Rondelet was over him still. He still believed that this man was a power. The first and the lifelong heroes are those of school and college. It is sad, indeed, when chance brings one face to face, in after years, with the great and gallant Captain of the school, to find that he is, after all, no greater than yourself, and, in fact, rather a mean sort of person. Next to the school hero comes he who was a hero among undergraduates. Alan believed formerly in that bright, clever, and conceited scholar who assumed every kind of knowledge, and talked like a Socrates. It was difficult not to believe in him still. He reflected that this would be his chance : he thought that it would be a great thing to let Rondelet prove his greatness to the outer world.

"I will guarantee the expense," he said at last, "for one year."

Paul Rondelet, shortly afterwards, stepped

out of his Fellowship with ease of mind.
The magazine was started.

It was exactly a year ago.   It ran for
nearly a year ; it contained the Poem of the
Sorrowful Young Man ; The Sonnet to Burne
Jones ; papers by Paul Rondelet on the
Orphic Myth, on the Bishops of the Renaissance, on certain obscure French poets, on
the Modern School of English Painting, on
the Italian Women of the Fifteenth Century,
on the Fall of the Church, and other papers.
Nobody except " the Circle" bought that
magazine; nobody advertised in it.   And
after ten months, for very shame, the
publishers advised Mr. Dunlop to pay the
editor his salary for the year and stop it.
Paul Rondelet now writes for the Daily
Press.   He contributes leaders to a penny
paper.   He glories in this occupation.   It is
not writing for the common herd any longer ;
it is "swaying the masses." His articles may
be known by frequent quotations, not from the
poets loved by the world, but from modern
writers, such as Morris and Rossetti; by
references to French writers not generally
known to mankind, such as Catulle Mendes,

Baudelaire, and Theodore de Banville; by the easy omniscience which is at home among pre - historic men, or among the scholars of the Renaissance or with the Darwinians; by an absolute inability to enter with sympathy into any phase of real life; and by an irrepressible tone of superiority. Whatever he says, this writer is always Paul Rondelet of Lothian.

CHAPTER XII.

"Now the nights are all passed over
Of our dreaming, dreams that hover
In a mist of fair, false things,
Nights afloat on wide wan wings."

THE day before the wedding.

In his two-roomed cottage, Alan awoke
with the feeling of gratitude that he should
only have one more night in that uncomfortable lean-to. The house which he had decided on occupying contained four rooms, and
they were larger.

It was meant as a surprise for Alma: the
furniture was ordered and ready, waiting to
be sent down: it was the furniture of the
Future: it came from an establishment recently started by two young ladies, one of
whom was a distinguished *alumnus* of Girton.

They had solemn eyes and touzly hair, and dressed to match their green and grey papers.

"I want furniture," said Alan, a little over-whelmed at being received by two figures which looked as if they had stepped straight down from the walls of the Grosvenor; "I want cottage furniture, which shall be beauti-ful as well as fit for its purpose."

"Furniture," suggested one, "which shall be a model and a lesson."

"Furniture," echoed the other lady-up-holsterer, "which shall be in harmony, not in contrast, with woodland nature.

"And it ought to be cheap," said Alan, "if it is to represent the ideal cottage furni-ture."

This suggestion, however, met with no re-sponse. The two-pair solemn eyes glared coldly upon the purchaser at the mention of cheapness.

"We will furnish your cottage for you," said one with severity. "When our designs are completed we will let you know. Good-morning."

Alan left the presence of these Parnassian cabinet-makers with humbled heart.

What a lovely cottage they would have made, but for circumstances which caused the dispersion of the things they had got together! It would have been divinely beautiful. The windows were to have diamond panes, in *grisaille*, to open on hinges : the rooms, each with a dado, were to be papered and painted in grey and green : Dutch tiles were to adorn the stoves, and the fenders were of brass : no carpets, of course, but matting in wonderful designs : cabinets for the inexpensive blue and white china : chairs in black wood and rush, with tables to correspond.

That cottage, for reasons to be detailed, was never furnished. The two touzly-haired, solemn eyed prophetesses of domestic art were obliged to content themselves with sending in their bill. This document caused Alan's strong frame to shiver and tremble as shivers the mighty oak under the cold breath that comes before a tempest.

Early in the morning Alan paid a visit to his betrothed. He came bearing gifts. They were plain and substantial things, such as the girl could not be expected to like—books, strong stuff for frocks, everything but what

she wanted, a laugh and a kiss, and the promise that she should be a lady.

As for laughing—if the bridegroom was so
solemn, what, in Heaven's name, would be the
husband ?

"Alma," he began, after a frigid touch of
the fingers, and in sepulchral tones, "tell me,
are you in the least degree distrustful of what
you are going to do ?"

"Oh ! no," she replied, with a little laugh,
which jarred upon him. She was thinking,
indeed, of something else that she was going
to do. " Not at all."

"It is not an easy part that you have
undertaken. Sometimes, my poor child, I
think it is too heavy a task for you."

" I shall manage it," she said, still thinking
of the other task.

"We will at once re-open the Public
Laundry, the Public Kitchen, the Public Baths,
the Good Liquor Bar, and the Co-operative
Store ; we will start on a new plan, the Village
Parliament, and we will improve the Library
and the Picture Gallery. Next winter we
will have the weekly dances begun again, and
we will make another attempt at a theatre."

"Yes," she said, with a curious smile, "all that will be very pleasant."

"Your duty," he went on, "will place you always in the company of the wives and girls."

"To be sure," said Alma, "if they like to follow my example, they can." An example, she thought, which would be one not entirely contemplated by her lover.

"We will have," he went on, "a quiet fortnight together by the sea-side, just to mature our plans and formulate our line of action."

"Yes," said Alma, wondering what on earth he meant by formulating a line of action. However, it would not matter.

He gave her, before he went away, a final *résumé* of his theories on social economy, which lasted for two hours. And then, to her great delight, he departed, promising to return in the evening.

I regret to state that as he closed the door, Alma so far retraced her steps in civilisation as to spring to her feet and . . . make a face at him. Quite like a vulgar Sunday-school girl.

Alan was anxious now to have the thing over, and to begin the new life on which he

staked so much. As for marriage, he confessed to himself that he was marrying the
wrong woman. But the only right woman
was Miranda, and she could not be expected
to live as Alma was going to live. The thing
to do was to drown selfish regrets and inclinations, and to persuade his wife to act her part
boldly and hopefully. Would Alma do that?

When he was gone, other visitors came.

First it was Tom Caledon. He had returned from town by the earliest train, and
was more than commonly cheerful.

"All is going well, Alma," he said. "Are
we quite alone here?"

"Yes; Miss Miranda leaves me here to
talk to Mr. Dunlop."

"Then . . . are you quite sure you can
keep a secret?"

"Girls," said Alma, with a little toss of
her pretty head, "keep their own secrets. It's
other people's they tell."

This remark will be found, on investiga-
tion, to contain the whole of feminine philosophy.

"Then, my dear child, you look really
much too pretty for Harry Cardew——"

"Oh! Mr. Caledon . . . don't."

"I will tell you what you are to do. Get up and be dressed by six. Come downstairs —you will find the back door open for you —at the garden-gate Harry will be waiting for you, and I shall have the cart in the road. You are sure you understand?"

"Quite sure," said Alma, repeating the lesson.

"One of the ladies of the Abbey"—here Tom turned very red—"will be with me. She is going too."

"Not the lady they call Desdemona? I should like her to go."

"No. Not Sister Desdemona. In fact it is . . . it is Miss Despard."

"I know Miss Nelly," said Alma. "I like her better than Miss Miranda. And I've seen her cry once."

What she meant was, that this little touch of human weakness seemed to bring Nelly nearer to herself. The queenly Miranda, she thought, *could* not cry.

"Oh! Mr. Caledon," Alma went on excitedly, "now it is coming I don't know how I feel. And to think of Mr. Dunlop's long face when he hears of it—and father's rage when *he* hears. He! he! he!"

"Yes," said Tom, with a queer smile, "there is plenty to think about. However, you think of your own triumph, Alma. Think of the people gaping when you get down— you and Harry—arm in arm; and when the vicar asks for the bride, and you will say, 'Thank you, Mr. Corrington, you are an hour too late."

"And shall we?" Alma asked, with eager eyes and parted lips. "Shall we?"

"To be sure we shall. Good-bye till to-morrow, Alma."

And then her mother came to see her.

"Bostock," she said, with the calmness of despair, "is blind drunk. He was drunk last night off brandy, and he's drunk this afternoon off hot gin-and-water a top of beer. What I shall do with Bostock now you are gone is more than I can tell. Dreadful, he carries on. Says he won't be safe till to-morrow. Cries when the drink's in him. What's the man got to be safe about?"

"I suppose, mother," said Alma the astute, "that he's got into a mess with his accounts.

You know father never can keep his accounts
the same as other people."

This was a kindly way of putting the fact
that Père Bostock, not for the first time, had
been cheating.

"And to think, Alma," her mother went
on, "to think that you are going to marry
the Squire.   Where's your wedding-dress,
girl?"

"Miss Dalmeny gave it me," said Alma,
jumping up. "Come to my bedroom, mother,
and see me try it on."   She led the way with
a little softening of her eyes as she thought of
Harry, and a twinkle as she thought of Mr.
Dunlop. "Won't Black Bess be in a rage
to-morrow!"

Then there was putting on and discussion
of the wedding-dress, which was a present
from Miranda.   And then, after judicious
criticism from the ex-lady's-maid, Alma resumed her morning frock, and Mrs. Bostock,
seating herself in the easy-chair, while her
daughter sat upon the bed, commenced a lecture on the duties of a married woman.

I am very sorry that there is no room for
this masterly discourse.   It was marked by

the solid good sense and by the practical experience which distinguished Mrs. Bostock.
The conclusion was as follows :

" As for his notions about living in a cottage and setting an example, and that, don't
put up your face against them at the beginning.
Say that you are setting an example. Then
you sit down and bide. When he's satisfied
that no good will come of an example—haven't
I been setting one for two and twenty years?
—he'll give it up. Only you bide, and you'll
live at Weyland Court like a lady. *Like* a
lady," she repeated, with dignified sadness,
" because a real lady you never can be."

" Nor don't want," said Alma, swinging her
feet, as she sat on the edge of the bed, in a
manner that went to her mother's heart.

" But you must try, so as not to make
people laugh at you."

Here Alma was seized with a fit of irrepressible laughing. It went on so long that
it nearly became hysterical.

" I can't help it, mother," she said at last,
partially recovering herself, " I can't help it,
not if I was in church I couldn't. Lord !
how everybody will look to-morrow !"

" Well, they know what to look for."

" Oh! no, they don't," cried Alma, laughing
again.   And I really do think that if her
mother had pressed her, Alma would there
and then have disclosed the whole plot and
ruined everything.   Because the thing which
tickled her was the thought of Alan's solemn
face and the consternation of her father.

Then her mother left her, promising to be
in good time at the church, and, above all, to
see that Bostock did not " take " anything before the ceremony.   She herself, she said,
had bought a new gown, and her husband a
new suit complete, for the occasion.   The
former she described at length, and was proceeding to describe her husband's coat, when
Alma again burst out into an uncontrollable
fit of laughing, insomuch that her mother
was fain to give her a glass of cold water,
undo her stays, and pat her on the back.

At luncheon there was no one but Miranda,
before whom the girl was generally afraid to
talk, and when she did, talked in bursts and
talked too much, as is the way with shy
people.   But this morning Alma felt a little
less afraid.   She was conscious that in a very

few hours Miss Dalmeny would regard her with changed, perhaps grateful feelings. This made her bold in speech.

" Do you think, Miss Dalmeny, that I am fitter to be a gentleman's wife than I was three weeks ago ?"

Miranda hesitated.

" But I know you don't," Alma went on, "and you believe that Mr. Dunlop's gone and made a mistake."

" That depends on yourself, Alma," said Miranda.

The bride-elect shook her head.

" No, it all depends on him. He asked me. I didn't want to marry him. And I never did fancy him. As for his caring about me, why he thinks more of your glove than of all me put together."

" But it is too late, Alma, to talk like that," said poor Miranda, with a blush. " You must think of nothing now but your husband's happiness."

Alma tossed her head and laughed. Thinking of Alan's long face on the morrow, she very nearly had another hysterical fit.

In the afternoon Desdemona drove over

from the Abbey, ostensibly to see Alma's wedding-dress.

" I know all about it, my dear," murmured Desdemona, in her sympathetic way, taking both the girl's hands in her own. " Tom Caledon has told me all about it. You will drive over to Athelston early and be married. And then you will drive back, under Harry Cardew's protection."

" Will you be there to see ?" cried Alma, her eyes flashing.

" Surely I will. I always intended to be there to see. Now, my dear. don't oversleep yourself. You are to get up at six and be quite ready."

" I must put on my wedding frock," said Alma eagerly.

"Of course, and here "—Desdemona opened a bundle and took out a long grey cloak—" here is something to put over it. I have thought that perhaps you might be met on your way by people coming from Athelston and recognised. That would not do. So I have brought you a thick veil ; mind you wear it in double folds until you are inside the church. And now, my dear, I think there is nothing else that I wanted to say, except "—here she produced a little box in white paper—" except these earrings, which I hope you will wear to be married in, from myself, and this necklace from Miss Despard. And oh! my dear child "—Desdemona's large eyes grew soft, and her voice, oh! so sympathetic—" I do so hope you will be happy, with the real man, the real man, of your own choice."

Alma was left before the glass trying on cloak, hood, necklace, and eardrops. She looked, she thought, too pretty to be a gamekeeper's wife. But that was being a lady, a rich, luxurious, and do-nothing fine lady, compared with living down in the village, doing your own washing, talking unintelligible sermons all the evening, and never, never to be out of the way of that grave face and those solemn searching eyes, always looking for the fruits of wisdom which Alma's little brain could never produce.

In the evening Alan came again, sat with her for two hours, and prosed to so awful an extent that the girl, whose nerves were for the time none of the strongest, had great difficulty in restraining the hereditary temper. It was fortunate that she overcame the temptation to spring to her feet, box her lover's ears, and tell him the whole story.

She did not, and was rewarded on his departure by his present of a gold watch and chain. She was so exasperated by his pictures of their coming felicity among the village wash-tubs that she hardly thanked him for it.

Finally, at ten o'clock Alma was able to go to her own room, and make her arrangements for the morning.

These were simple. She laid out her wedding dress, put the trinkets and watch on the table so that she should not forget them, and laid her head upon the pillow in happy anticipation of the morrow.

In the conservatory of the Abbey stood Tom and Nelly. There might have been other pairs in that extensive and beautiful house of flowers, but this couple were apart apparently examining a splendid palm. But they held each other by the hand in a manner quite unbecoming the dignity of botany.

" To-morrow morning, Nelly," murmured
Tom, looking more foolish than one would
have believed possible in any man.

" To-morrow morning, Tom," murmured
Nelly, raising her lustrous eyes to meet his,
and looking softly, sweetly and sympathetically
beautiful. Why under these circumstances
does man always look like an ass, and woman
like an angel ? I know of nothing to make a
bridegroom assume the expression of a fool,
or a bride that of a superior being.

Then Nelly produced a letter.

" See, Tom," she said, her eyes brimming
with *malice* and yet her lips a little trembling ;
" this letter came this morning. And I think
that, as Desdemona would say, it looks like
improving the situation. Listen.

" ' Dear Eleanour '—I suppose you hardly
knew, you ignorant Tom, that my real name
is Eleanour. Papa always called me Nelly,
though—' I can hardly tell you how greatly I
have been shocked by a discovery made yes-
terday evening. I am only astonished that
you with your opportunities did not find it
out before. I at once wrote a letter to you
enjoining immediate return home, but it

was then too late for the evening post'—
what luck, Tom! 'My discovery was that
this Mr. Roger Exton is ACTUALLY a married
man. A more heartless case of deliberate
deception I have never known. He has been
everywhere supposed to be unmarried; he
has been taken to meet dozens of girls; he
was called the Assam Nabob; he was received with the consideration due to a man
who is at once rich and comparatively young
and unmarried. Your Aunt Mildred'—she
has daughters, too, Tom—'discovered it, and
immediately communicated the news to me.
He is married to a half-caste, not a Ranee,
a Begum, or an Indian person covered with dia-
monds whom one would be proud to take out
in the evening, but of quite common mercan-
tile extraction, probably a Heathen. Wickedness and selfishness of this kind make one
despair of human nature. And this very
morning, the villain had the effrontery to call
upon me. I hope and believe'—think upon
this, Tom—'that I behaved as an offended
English mother should. I do not *think* he
will venture here again. Meantime, through
this impostor's arts, you have lost the whole

of the summer, and I am afraid got yourself talked about '—I am afraid I shall be, Tom, if I have not already. 'I am, however, going to Hastings, and shall take Weyland Court on my way there. You can be ready to leave that place, which I am very sorry you ever saw, on Saturday. I shall stop at Athelston, and drive over to take you away.' Only just in time, Tom."

"Plenty of time," said Tom.

"Poor mamma! I am sorry for her; and she was so ambitious for me too, Tom. I wonder what she will say. Are you afraid? Papa once said, after he lost money at Newmarket, that there were moments when she was scathing in her wrath."

Last scene of this anxious day.

It is eleven o'clock. Tom has stolen away from the Abbey, and has sought Alan in his cottage.

He found him restless and anxious, pacing the narrow limits of his little room.

"I came—I came," Tom stammered, "to wish you happiness."

"Thank you," said Alan shortly, and continued his promenade.

"I wonder if you feel happy," Tom went on.

" No, I do not," said Alan, more shortly.

" Do you think that you have made a mistake ? Alan, perhaps it is not too late even now."

" I cannot discuss it, Tom. Mistake or not, it is made. Too late now for anything."

" I am sorry," said Tom. "And if it were not too late, Alan ?"

CHAPTER XIII.

"Go, waken Juliet; go and trim her up :
    Make haste : the bridegroom he is come already."

THE first person to rise at Dalmeny Hall on
the wedding morning was the bride. Alma
Bostock sprang from her bed rosy-fingered
as Aurora, while the clock was striking five.
She had one short hour for the most important
toilette she would ever make. She was accustomed to rapidity in these things, however,
and it wanted yet a quarter to six when she
stood before the cheval glass—of which she
will ever after retain a longing memory—
complete in all her bridal glories, attired for
the greatest event in a woman's life, and
ejaculating with a gasp something like Jack
Horner, "Oh! what a pretty girl I am!"

Her dress was a pearl-grey muslin costume,

a real lady's dress, with trimmings such as
she had only heretofore seen in the drapers'
shops at Athelston. A few red ribbons Alma
thought would have improved the dress, but
doubtless her mother knew best, and she had
decided against them. To be sure Alma had
a fine rosy cheek of her own, and could dis-
pense with more colour. Round her neck
was a white lace *fichu*, real lace, also part of
a proper lady's dress. Her bonnet was of
white silk, a marvel and a wonder of a bonnet, the like of which Alma had never even
dreamed of; her gloves, of pale lavender, had
five buttons on each wrist, and each ad-
ditional button went straight to Alma's heart.
She had on the earrings which Desdemona
gave her, and the necklace which Miss
Despard gave her, and the watch and chain
which Mr. Dunlop gave her—the last were
superfluous, but Alma could hardly be expected to know that. So attired, she stood
before the glass and cried aloud, " What a
pretty girl I am !"

Outside, the morning sunshine of August
lay upon the garden and the park, and had
already dried up the morning dew ; below

her window the gardener's boy sharpened his
scythe musically, and then began again his
low and gentle sh—sh—sh over the lawn;
in the woods and coppice behind the garden
there was the late song of the blackbird, the
carol of the thrush, the melancholy coo of the
woodpigeon : as she opened the window there
poured in a breeze laden with all kinds of
perfumes from the garden.   These things
were habitual to her ; she noticed none of
them, just as the Oreads and Dryads, the
Wood-nymphs, Fountain-nymphs, and Moun-
tain-nymphs, who lived habitually amid the
most beautiful scenery, took no notice of it.
At least we may suppose so, because they
have passed away without so much as a line
of poetry to indicate their joy in flowers,
leaves, springtide, and summer.

The gracious influences of the morning air,
the recollection of Miranda's kindness, the
thought of Alan Dunlop's pain, the knowledge of her father's reliance in their marriage
to suit his own purpose, had no weight with
Alma.   She took no heed of them.   She
thought only that she loved Harry, who was
a real man ; that her father's discomfiture

would be a sight to see, and Mr. Dunlop's
long face a most comical and surprising thing
to witness ; and oh! to get away from that
grave face ; to be no longer haunted with
unintelligible sermons.   At any cost, she
thought, even at the cost of marrying a poor
man.   But Harry Cardew had money saved,
and as Harry said, they could go to Canada,
buy a piece of land, and farm it for themselves.   She would be no poorer than she had
been, and as for her father's nonsense about
his being a gamekeeper, everybody respected
Harry far more, she knew very well, than they
respected Stephen Bostock.

Alma did not look very far ahead.   Had
she desired what Chaucer thought women
love most—power—she would have taken
Alan.   For she could have ruled him by a
terrible weapon which she possessed, whose
force she did not know, her coarse and violent
temper.   Scenes which to her meant nothing
would have been death to him.   He would
have conceded anything to escape torture of
ear and eye, while Alma would be merely enjoying the freedom of her tongue.

But in marrying Harry she was marrying

her master. This she knew in some vague way. She feared Mr. Dunlop because he was a gentleman; she feared Harry—only in this case the fear was not a terrible but a delightful thing—because he was strong, and because he was masterful.

It was six o'clock. Alma took one final lingering gaze of admiration in the glass, huddled on the long cloak, tied the blue veil in many folds over her bonnet *à l'Américaine*, and thus disguised, opened the door cautiously.

Not a soul was stirring in the house. She slid down the stairs as noiselessly as Godiva, stepped cautiously to the garden door, in which, according to promise, she found the key, opened it, and so out into the garden.

Her heart was beating fast now. She was actually carrying her dream of revenge into effect. As she closed the door behind her it seemed as if she was cutting off the last chance of reconsideration. She thought with a little sinking of the heart of what might have been, Weyland Court, ladyhood, carriages, endless frocks. But then—that grave and solemn man ; and no Weyland Court at all certain, but only misery in a labourer's cottage.   She set her lips with determination, and ran down the steps.

On the lawn the under-gardener Robert looked up and grinned surprise.

" Good-morning, Robert," said Alma with great sweetness.   " If you see Miss Dalmeny, will you tell her that I have gone to see my mother ?"

" I'll tell her," said Robert.

" And you are going to the wedding, Robert ?"

He was—everybody was going there : all the world was going, Robert among them. She laughed lightly, and ran down the garden walk.   Outside the little gate she found Harry Cardew waiting for her, and looked up in his face laughing for fun.

Men are so different from women.   There was no mirth at all in his face, but a grave sadness, which disappointed her.   But he took her in his arms and kissed her through the veil.   She noticed, too, that he was smartened up ; had on what appeared to be an entirely new suit, in which he did not appear at ease.

" I am sorry," he said—" I'm main sorry for Master Alan. It seems a poor return for all these years, and me to have gone about in the woods with him when we was both boys and all."

· " Perhaps," said Alma, " I'd better go back and wait in my room till ten o'clock."

" No," said Harry grimly. " I've got you this time, Master Alan or not; and I'll keep you. Come along, Alma. There's only one who loves you that truly as dare all to have you."

Masterfulness such as this takes a girl's breath away. However, Alma came out that fine morning on purpose to be run away with.

From the garden-gate to the road was a matter of a hundred yards or so. Alma looked back a dozen times, pretending fear of pursuit. Harry marched on disdainful. It would have been a strong band of pursuers to balk him of his bride when he had got so far.

Then they crossed the stile and were in the road.

" Mr. Tom said he'd meet us hereabouts," said Harry, " at six."

It was not the high-road from Weyland to
Athelston, but a winding little by-way, once a
bridle-road for pack-horses, cattle and pedes-
trians, before the days of high-roads and
coaches—a by-way arched over and shaded
with trees—a way on which there was
little chance of meeting any of the Weyland
people.

As Harry spoke Tom came driving along
the road.

He was in a dog-cart. Beside him, dressed
in simple morning hat and summer jacket,
was Miss Despard.

Nelly jumped down and ran to greet Alma,
kissing her on both cheeks, to her great
wonder.

"My dear child," she said, "we are both
in exactly the same case." What *did* she
mean? "Jump up quick, lest they run after
us and catch us. No"—for Alma was about
to mount behind—"you sit in the front beside
Tom, and for Heaven's sake keep your veil
down. It would never do for you to be recognised."

This arrangement effected, they drove on,
and Alma observed that Mr. Caledon was as

grave and subdued as her Harry—a very re-markable circumstance. Tom, indeed, spoke hardly at all during the drive; only he said to Alma once, in jerks:

"I saw Mr. Dunlop last night. Did not tell him what was going to happen. Very good thing we stopped it."

"Father wanted it," said Alma, who was now horribly frightened.

Harry, behind, did not volunteer one single word to Nelly. Probably he was afraid of ladies. Alma was much the more finely dressed of the two, and yet, somehow, he had no fear of her. Fine feathers, he re-flected, being a naturalist, make fine birds, but they do not make lady-birds.

It was half-past seven when they drove through the streets of Athelston, clattering over the cobbled stones of the quiet old cathedral town, which was beginning to get itself awakened. But the shops were not open, and only the servants were at the street doors.

Tom drove to the stable-yard of the hotel, and handed over the trap to a boy.

"Now, Harry," he said, "Miss Despard

and I are going to do exactly the same thing
as you and Alma.   Let us make our way to
the church."

Not one of the little party spoke as they
walked along the empty streets.   Both the
girls were inclined to cry, and the men looked
as if they were marching to battle.

The church was a great solitude : nobody
in it but the verger and an old woman, one
of those ancient dames who are to be found
attached to every church all over the world,
who never grow any older and were certainly
never young.   They pass their days in the
church ; they regard it as a private place of
residence, subject only to periodical invasion
from the outside world.   Some of them, I
dare say, sleep in the church as well.

Alma stopped to untie her veil and throw
off her cloak.   Then she took Harry's arm
and walked after Tom and Nelly as proudly
in her splendid dress as if she was under a
thousand eyes.   As they reached the altar
a clergyman came out of the vestry, the clerk
got within the rails, the verger stood in readiness to give away the bride, and the marriage
ritual began.   In Nelly's cheeks was a spot of

burning red : her eyes were downcast, and she trembled. Alma's eyes glittered bright and hard ; she did not tremble, but she thought of the awful Row that was going to happen, she pictured Alan waiting for her at the altar of Weyland Church, grave and solemn; and she almost began to giggle again, when she ought to have been listening to the words of the service.

" For better, for worse." Their hands were joined, their union consecrated, their marriage actually accomplished.

It was all over, then. Tom and Harry Cardew were now, as the Prayer-book reminded them at the close of the service, like Peter the Apostle, who was " himself a married man."

They went into the vestry and signed the registers. Thomas Aubrey Caledon, bachelor, and Eleanour Despard, spinster. Harry Cardew, bachelor, and Alma Bostock, spinster. It took ten minutes to get through these formalities, the two brides looking furtively at each other, wondering if it was really true, and feeling the ring upon their fingers.

"Now," said Tom, distributing largesse
quite beyond his income to all the minor
actors in the drama, "Now, my dear wife"—
Nelly started and gasped—"and Alma, as, I
suppose, we have none of us had any breakfast, and we have got a good deal to get
through this morning, let us go back to the
hotel."

Here they presently found a royal breakfast, though I fear scant justice was done to
it by the brides. And when Tom poured
out the champagne and drank to his wife and
to Alma, and when Harry, the shamefaced
Harry, raised his glass to his wife and said,
"Your health, Alma, my dear, and my true
service to you, Mrs. Caledon," Nelly fairly
broke down and burst into tears. She was
joined by Alma, partly for sympathy and
partly because she, too, was agitated by the
mingled emotions of joy, terror, and mis-
giving.

CHAPTER XIV.

"Next morn, betimes, the bride was missing ;
The mother screamed, the father chid,
'Where can this idle wench be hid ?'"

DESDEMONA, on the fateful morning, invited
herself to breakfast at the Hall. When she
arrived at nine, Miranda was already in the
breakfast-room. Alma, needless to say, had
not yet appeared.

"She is naturally a long time dressing,"
said Miranda.

"Quite naturally," said Desdemona, un-
blushing.

At a quarter-past nine Miranda went in
search of her. There was no Alma in the
room at all. Perhaps she was in the garden.

On inquiry under-gardener Robert deposed
that at six o'clock or thereabouts Miss Alma

came into the garden and said she was going to her mother.

" It shows very proper feeling," said Miranda.

" It does," said Desdemona. By this time she was quite hardened.

Alan was coming for his bride at ten, and at half-past ten the wedding was to take place. There was, therefore, no time to be lost. Miranda sent a pony-carriage to bring her back immediately. Then Alan came, before his time. He was pale and nervous; his look was heavy and grave. Miranda's eyes filled with involuntary tears as she met him.

And then began the wedding-bells, clashing and pealing. They heard them, too, the runaways, driving back to Weyland, on the road just outside Athelston—clang, clash, clang. Joy-bells to greet the brides. Clang, clash—and every bell striking upon Alan's nerves like the hammer of a torturer. Clang, clash. Desdemona shrank into the recess of the oriel window, thinking of what had happened. The bells made her tremble lest the grand *coup* should have failed. Clang, clash

—and at the Abbey the Monks of Thelema looked mournfully at each other, to think of such a wilful throwing away of a man, and the Sisters shed tears, and Lord Alwyne rose hastily from the breakfast-table and sought solitude, for his faith in Desdemona was sorely tried.

Clang, clash, clang, and all the village and the people from the country-side, rich and poor, gentle and simple, are gathering in the church and crowding in the churchyard. Among them are Black Bess and that other girl who assisted at the Judgment of Paris, their hearts bursting with jealousy at the great fortune that had befallen her who carried off the golden apple.

The Abbey of Thelema was not without representatives. All the Sisters arrived soon after this, accompanied by some of the Monks. They sent their band, which was stationed on the village green, outside the churchyard, to discourse triumphal music. They provided bunting and Venetian masts to make the village gay. Also, they had erected a vast marquee, in which all the villagers were to be regaled with beef and

pies and beer at noon, and again at nine, at
the charges of the Abbey.   In the evening
there were to be fire-works.   All was joy save
in the village Library, where the librarian,
little thin pale-faced Prudence, sat in a corner
quite alone among her books, weeping for the
future of her Prophet, the best and noblest
of all prophets.

The church was full and the churchyard
overflowing and the village green thronged,
when, at about twenty minutes past ten, the
father of the bride made his appearance.   It
was the proudest moment of his life.   He
was accompanied, of course, by Mrs. Bostock.
Alma, it was understood, would be brought
to the church—a departure from ordinary
rule—by the bridegroom and Miss Dalmeny,
who would act as bridesmaid.   Mr. Caledon,
it was also whispered, would be best-man.
Harry Cardew, said Black Bess, showed his
good sense by staying away.   Mrs. Bostock
wore her new dress, looking rather ashamed
of her prominent position.   Her husband, on
the other hand, attired in a large brown coat
with a fancy waistcoat, the garb, he considered, of the well-to-do farmer, bore him-

self bravely. He had studied his expression
before a looking-glass. It conveyed, though
he did not mean all of it, a curious mixture
of pride, cunning, humility, and self-satisfac-
tion. He wished his expression to say, as
clearly as waggling head, half-closed eye, and
projecting chin could speak, " Behold in me,
ladies and gentlemen, a man whom merit
alone has raised to this dizzy height of greatness."

Then the bells clashed and clanged their
loudest : and the band on the village green
played in emulation of the bells : and everybody began to look at the clock and to expect
the bride.

Half-past ten. The vicar was already in
the vestry, attired in his robes : they had
made a lane in the churchyard, along which
the bridal procession should pass : children
were there with baskets full of roses to strew
before the feet of the bride.

A quarter to eleven. Why did they not
come ?

Ten minutes to eleven. There was a
sound of wheels outside : the bells suddenly
stopped : the band was silent : and then there

was a great shout : and everybody stood up :
and the vicar came from the vestry and passed
within the altar rails.

Well! why did they not come into the
church ?

The reason was, that although the bride
was there, she had not come with the bridegroom, nor in the manner expected.

Another shout, and then the people in the
church who were nearest the door began to
slip out : they were followed by those nearest
to them, and so on, until the church was
finally deserted except by Mr. and Mrs. Bostock and the vicar. Outside there was a
great clamour, with laughing and shouting.

" Whatever can have happened, Stephen ?"
whispered his wife.

" Nothing can't have happened," said her
husband, sitting down doggedly.

Then Mrs. Bostock saw Mr. Caledon walking rapidly up the aisle, and she knew that
something had happened.

Tom went first to the vicar, to whom he
whispered a few words, which had the effect
of inducing his reverence to retire immediately
to the vestry. Then Tom turned to the Bailiff.

"Whatever has happened, Mr. Caledon?" cried the poor wife, in dire apprehension.

"Nothing, I tell you," interrupted her husband, with a pallid face. "Nothing can't have happened. They've all gone outside to see my beautiful little gell. That's what has happened. You and your happening!"

"Your daughter, Mr. Bostock," said Tom gravely, "is already married!"

Mrs. Bostock knew instantly to whom. Her husband gazed stupidly. He did not comprehend at all.

"She was married this morning at Athelston. I was present. She was married to Harry Cardew, the gamekeeper."

Tom felt pity for the man. He knew—everybody knew—that Bostock was a vulgar cheat who had intended to *exploiter* Alan as much as he could. Yet no one could behold the look of livid despair which fell upon the Bailiff's face without pity. No matter what his deserts were: his sufferings at that moment were too great for him to bear.

It was well that Alma did not witness the despair which she had brought upon her father.

He did not speak : he did not swear : he
only sat down and gasped, his eyes staring
wide, his mouth open, his red cheeks grew
suddenly pale.

"Go away, Mr. Caledon," said his wife
gently.   "Keep her out of her father's sight.
Go away.   Don't stay here."

Tom left them.

"Come, Stephen," she said, "let us go out
by the vestry and get home."

He only moaned.

"Stephen, come !"

He made no reply.   She sat beside him,
patient, expectant.   Half an hour passed.
Then he shivered and pulled himself together.

"Ruin," he said, "ruin and disgrace.
That's what it means." He wiped his clammy
brow, and rose up, his hands shaking as he
stood.

"I shall go home."

He marched straight down the aisle, followed by his wife. Outside, the villagers and
their friends were all on the green and in the
street, talking and laughing.   Their laughter
was hushed as they made way for the stricken

man, who walked heavily leaning on his stick, and the shamefaced woman who walked beside her husband.

When he reached home, he put the pony in his light cart, went into the room which he used as an office, collected all the farm books and placed them in the cart.

" I shall not be home to-night," he said, " but I'll write you a letter."

He drove away, and Mrs. Bostock, left alone and fearful, sat down and cried.

The Bailiff drove to Athelston, visited the bank, and drew out all the money then standing to his name, belonging partly to himself and partly to the farm. He then took the next train to London.

Two letters arrived from him the next day. That addressed to the Squire began with condolences. He pitied, he said, the misfortune which had befallen him, and lamented the wickedness to which he had fallen a victim. As regarded his daughter's husband, he supposed that Mr. Dunlop could do nothing less than instantly deprive the villain of his post and drive him from the estate ; and he expressed a fervent hope that the joint

career of bride and bridegroom would shortly
end in a ditch by death from inanition.   For
himself he begged a holiday of a month or
so, to recruit his shattered nerves.   He had
taken with him, he went on to say, the farm
books, so as not to be idle during this vacation, and in order to present them on his
return as accurate as he could wish to see.
To his wife he wrote simply that he didn't
intend to return for a spell.

He has not yet returned : nor have the
books been sent back : nor does any one
know why all the money was taken from the
bank.

Alma's *coup* was so far a failure, that she
did not see her father's face.   But it was
magnificent to stand on the village green beside her Harry, dressed as she was, with all
her fine presents glittering upon her, and to
watch in the crowd, as envious as she could
wish, Black Bess herself and that other girl.
It was great grandeur, too, that beside her
stood her sister-bride, the newly-made Mrs.
Caledon.

If she had married a gamekeeper, she had
jilted a squire : it was done under the protec-

tion and wing of one of the ladies of the Abbey : and as no one yet knew that Miss Despard had also that morning "changed her condition," all the sympathy, all the glory, was for herself.

Then Tom came out of the church : they mounted into their places again, and drove away through the Venetian masts and among the waving flags, while the band struck up a wedding march, and all the people shouted and laughed and waved their caps.

This time to Dalmeny Hall.

Alma was again disappointed. Mr. Caledon invited Harry and herself to wait in one of the morning-rooms, while he sought Alan.

He found him with Miranda and Desdemona. They were waiting. Something must have happened, because the bells, which had ceased for a while, had again burst forth in maddening peals.

"Alan," he said, with hesitation—" Alan, I wonder if you will forgive me."

" What is it, Tom ?" cried Miranda, springing to her feet. Desdemona only smiled.

" I told you last night, Alan, that I was sorry that you thought it too late to break off your engagement. I am here this morning to tell you that it is too late now for you to marry Alma."

" Why is it too late ?" asked Alan.

" Because she is already married," replied Tom. "She was married this morning—I was present—to Harry Cardew."

" My gamekeeper ?"

" And her former lover."

" Her former lover ? Could not some one have told me ?" he asked.

" I could," said Desdemona boldly, "or Tom. But Harry insisted that we should not. We devised, Tom and I between us, this means of rescuing you and the girl from sorrow and misery. No one else knew."

" Yes," said Nelly, who had joined them, I knew. Tom told me last night."

" Why did not Alma tell me ?"

" Because she was afraid of you," said Tom : " because her father was mad to have the match for his own ends : because——"

"Well," said Alan, "never mind the reasons. Where are they ?"

" They are in the breakfast-room."

" I should not like to see them," said Alan.

"I think it would be better not. Go, Tom, and tell Harry—and Alma too—that had I known the truth, this . . . this confusion would have been avoided. Tell him, too, that I desire he will take a month's holiday away from the place."

"Will you forgive us, Alan?" asked Desdemona.

He looked round him with a strange air of relief. And as he stood there, trying to realise what had befallen him, he smiled as a thought struck him.

"It is too ridiculous," he said, taking her proffered hand. "I suppose I ought to be the best laughed-at man in all England. Tom, the people were to have a big feed to-day. Do not let that be stopped. Send word that they are to drink the health of the bride and bridegroom, Alma and Harry Cardew."

"Then we are forgiven?" said Desdemona, again.

There was no time for Alan to reply, for the door opened—

"Mrs. Despard and Lord Alwyne Fontaine."

"I rejoice," said Mrs. Despard—she was a

17—2

tall lady of resolute figure, Roman nose, long chin, and manly bearing—not the least like Nelly—" I rejoice—kiss me, my dear;" this was to Nelly, who dutifully greeted her parent, and then retired, trembling, to the contiguity of Tom—"that I arrive at a moment when we all ought to rejoice. I have just heard, Mr. Dunlop, that your un-Christian design has been frustrated."

"Yes," said Alan simply.

"How do you do, Miranda?" Mrs. Despard ignored Desdemona and Tom altogether. " I think, however, that one example in the—so-called—Abbey is enough. I am come to take my daughter away. Are you ready, Eleanour?"

At any other time Nelly would have replied that she was quite ready, even though nothing at all had been packed. Now she fell back, literally, upon Tom, who, with his arm round her waist, stepped to the front.

"Nelly is not ready, Mrs. Despard."

" What, sir?"

"You come a couple of hours too late. We were married this morning, Nelly and

I, at eight o'clock, in the parish church of Athelston."

They were all startled, especially Desdemona, who really had known nothing of this.

" Eleanour," cried Mrs. Despard, turning very red, " is this true ?"

" Quite true, mamma," said Nelly, trembling.

" You knew of this, Miranda ?"

" No, indeed," said Miranda ; "this is the first I have heard of it."

Tom looked to be " scathed," like the late lamented Colonel. Nothing of the kind. Mrs. Despard was not equal to an emergency of such magnitude. She only dropped her head for a few moments into her handkerchief, as if she were in church, and then lifting it, mildly remarked :

" I have been much to blame. I might have known that a place with no regular chaperon "—she turned an icy glance upon Desdemona—" where the owner of the house was disgracing himself by an engagement with a milkmaid "—she was warming up, Nelly thought—" where he set the example

of living in a smock-frock on cold boiled
pork——"

"No," said Alan, smiling; "I deny the
cold boiled pork."

"Where one of the guests—I will not call
them Brothers after the blasphemous fashion
of the place—was a married man pretending
to be a bachelor ; when another was . . .
was "—here her eyes met those of Tom, and
her language assumed greater elevation—
"the penniless and unprincipled adventurer
who once before endeavoured to shipwreck
my daughter's happiness . . . considering, I
say, these things, I have principally myself
to blame.   Eleanour, when I can forgive you
I will write to you.   Lord Alwyne, would
you kindly take me to my carriage ?"

Well, they were all a little scathed—from
Desdemona to Nelly.   But Miranda rushed
for her, so to speak, and the kissing and the
hand-shaking, and the good-wishes went far
to dry poor Nelly's tears, and make her look
forward with a cheerful hope to the day of
forgiveness.

This day was materially accelerated by
Lord Alwyne.

"Your attitude, my dear madam," he said with much show of sympathy, on the stairs, "is entirely what we should have expected of you. Indeed, I would not, if I may advise, be too ready to forgive my dear little friend, your daughter. Disobedience to parents is greatly prevalent among us. Think of my son Alan."

"It is, Lord Alwyne," she said with a sob, "it is; but after all my plans for her success! But you knew her father. She inherits the Colonel's yielding disposition."

"Too true," moaned Lord Alwyne—they were now at the carriage-door. "Meanwhile, my dear madam, I may tell you that Tom Caledon, your son-in-law, has this day conferred a service on the Fontaines which it will be difficult to repay. He has kept the dairymaid out of the family. If there is any one single post left in the country which a minister can give away, and for which there is no competitive examination, I shall ask for that post for him. I write to-day to the Duke, my brother, telling him all!.

"Position and income," said Mrs. Despard, visibly softening, "can ill replace a daughter's confidence and trust. You know not, Lord Alwyne, a mother's feelings."

The influence of the head of the House of Fontaine, when the Conservatives are in, is very great. They did say that the appointment of Tom Caledon to that Commissionership was a job. I do not know. As no one ever proposed that I should have the place for myself, I am prepared to believe that Tom is quite as able to discharge the duties as any of the hundred men who wanted it. At all events he is there, and I am sure that the official twelve hundred a year added to his own modest income will go a long way towards reconciling his mother-in-law with her daughter.

There was a beautiful scene in the marquee : Tom Caledon, without Nelly, stood at the head of the table, glass in hand. At his right, Alma, in her wedding-dress ; beside her, her husband, shamefaced ; behind her, murmuring sympathy and support, Desdemona ; all the village at the tables, whereon are the remnants of the pies. Men and women, boys and girls, all are there — the

young man they call Will-i-am, old Methu-
selah Parr, the cobbler, the schoolmaster,
Black Bess, and Prudence Driver, looking
happy again. In the doorways some of the
ladies of the Abbey; the vicar and his
daughters ; Lord Alwyne, and strangers.

"Health !" shouts Tom Caledon ; "health
and happiness to Harry Cardew and his wife!"

"Tell me, Miranda," said Alan, when they
were left alone, "are you as pleased as the
rest with the finish of my engagement ?"

"Yes, Alan," she replied frankly.

"I must not make a mistake a second
time," he said ; "Fortune never forgives a
second blunder."

"No," said Miranda, smiling, and not immediately seeing the drift of this observation.

"But," he said, holding out both his hands,
"there is only one way of preventing that
folly. Miranda, will you help me ?"

Who after this could ever say that Miranda was cold, or Alan frigid ?

I should like to explain that Alma, so far,

has been a model wife. To be sure she is horribly afraid of her husband, who, now that he has given up gamekeeping and taken Bostock's farm, is more masterful than ever. Her mother lives with her ; and her mother's counsels, seeing that Harry is so steady a husband, make in the direction of obedience. Harry, perhaps, remembers Desdemona's advice.

CHAPTER THE LAST.

" Cras amet qui nunquam amavit,
    Quique amavit, cras amet."

THAT evening, while the villagers rejoiced in
unlimited beer, and danced after their fashion
upon the village green; and while the un-
wonted rocket brought the flush of rapture to
the village beauty's cheek ; while Black Bess,
with the other who had missed the apple,
consoled themselves with the thought that
after all *she*, meaning Alma, had only married
a gamekeeper, there was high revelling at the
Abbey.   Here Desdemona improvised what
she called a Farewell Chapter.   The nature of the ceremonies which attended a
Function of the Order has already been
indicated.   This, however, surpassed all previous ceremonies.   After the opening rites.

with the organ, Sister Desdemona presented
to the Abbess, Brother Lancelot and Sister
Rosalind, as two members of the Order about
to quit the convent on entering into the holy
state of wedlock—a case, she pointed out,
already provided for by the Founder.   Then
Desdemona read in the Great Book of Ritual
the following passage :

"'Wherefore, should the time come when
any Brother of the Abbey has a mind to go
out of it, he may carry with him one of the
Sisters, namely her who has already accepted
him as her servant, and they shall be married together.   And let all the world know
that if they have formerly lived in the Abbey
in devotion and amity, still more shall they
continue that love in marriage ; and they
shall love each other to the end of their
days as much as on the first day of their
wedding.'

"It is in reliance on this rule, my Lady,"
said Desdemona, ignoring the fact that Tom
and Nelly were already, and secretly, married, "that our Brother and our Sister seek
the permission of the Order to leave the
Abbey."

Miranda, with great dignity, asked if any Brother or Sister had reason to allege why this permission should not be granted.

After an interval, she deputed the Public Orator to speak for her.

Brother Hamlet, who spoke with great hesitation, which was naturally attributed to the *contretemps* of the morning, pronounced the farewell oration prescribed, he said, though no one had ever heard of it before, by the Rules of the Order of Thelema. I can only find room for the peroration :

" Lastly, Brother Lancelot and Sister Rosalind, you have heard the gracious words of our Founder. Go forth from the Abbey with the congratulations and wishes of those to whom you have been indeed brother and sister : may your love continue and grow : forget not ever the Abbey of Thelema : remember in the outer world the teaching of the Order : teach those who come after that to gentlehood and courtesy, there is no law but one, '*Fay ce que vouldras.*' Do what honour bids."

He ceased. Sister Desdemona stepped from her desk and solemnly received from the pair, who stood before the Lady Abbess, the hood, the gown, and the crimson cord of the Fraternity. Two of the Sisters, as Nelly resigned these monastic badges, robed her from head to foot in a bridal veil.

Then the band began a low prelude, and the choir sang the Farewell Song :

> " You, who have learned and understood
>   The master's rules that bind us,
> And chosen, as the chiefest good,
>   The end that he designed us ;
> Who hand-in-hand before us stand
>   In sober guise, not fiction :
> Take, ere you part, from heart to heart,
>   This Chapter's benediction.

> " Think, Brother, whom our Sister chose
>   Her servant in devotion,
> Love's service never flags but grows
>   Deep as the deepest ocean.
> To thee we trust her, taught we know,
>   In this, the Master's College,
> Still to obey her lord, while thou
>   Shalt still thy Queen acknowledge.

> " With tears we greet thee, Sister sweet,
>   Lady of grace and beauty,
> To whom love draws by nature's laws,
>   Whose service is but duty.
> Be thine to make the wedded life,
>   As this our cloister, sunny.

Be mistress still as well as wife,
    Be every moon of honey.

" So fond farewells : thy vacant cells
    Await a fit successor,
For Rosalind needs must we find
    No meaner and no lesser.

" Farewell, farewell : go forth in peace
    To sweet and happy living ;
Let flowers grow your feet below ;
Your path be bright with hope and light ;
Let sunshine stay beside your way—
    Your years one long thanksgiving."

The choir ceased. Then, as the last bars pealed and echoed among the black rafters of the roof, the Public Orator took Nelly by the hand and led her to the throne of the Abbess. Miranda raised the bridal veil, and gave her Sister the farewell kiss. Tears stood in her eyes, and Nelly was crying quite freely and naturally. Each of the Sisters in turn kissed the bride, and the Brothers kissed her hand. Then a similar ceremony—*mutatis mutandis* —was undergone by Tom, Brother Lancelot no longer. Then they waited a moment while a procession formed, and then the organ struck up the wedding march, and the

Chapter was finished. First marched the
stewards and clerks of the Order, followed by
the choir. Then followed, two by two, the
Fraternity of Thelema. Then came pages
bearing on crimson cushions the gifts of the
Monks and Sisters to the bride—the notice
was so short that they could give her nothing
more than jewels and trinkets, but these made
a pretty show. The wedded pair walked
next; and last, followed only by the pages who
bore her train, came Miranda, led by Alan.

As they passed the bust of the Master, the
electric light fell full upon the kindly features
and the wise smile, and on his lips seemed
to play the words which were written in
gold below :

" FAY CE QUE VOULDRAS."

The dinner which followed was graced by
as many guests as could be got together at a
short notice. Tom sat next to Miranda,
beside him his bride ; next to her, Lord
Alwyne, in great contentment, looking, as he
told everybody himself, ten years younger.
Alan sat next to Miranda ; opposite her,
Desdemona. As for Nelly, she had left off

crying, and was now, so far from being cast down by the maternal wrath, shyly but radiantly happy. It was a quiet banquet; the band played wedding music selected by Cecilia, the boys sang four-part songs which bore upon love's triumphs; yet all the Brothers looked constrained. There were only two exceptions. Tom, whose honest face betokened gratification of the liveliest kind, and Alan, who was transformed.

Yes; the heavy pained look was gone from his brow; his deep eyes were lit with a new and strange light; his face was wreathed with smiles.

"Daddy Graveairs," said his father, after gazing furtively at him, "is reflecting that he is well rid of the dairymaid. I think we shall not see much more of the smock-frock. Gad! the fellow is only five-and-twenty or so yet. What an age! And what a rollicking youngster he will be at fifty!"

It was Lord Alwyne who proposed the health of the bride and bridegroom. He surpassed himself.

Then came Desdemona's turn. It seemed as if nobody could be so happy as Desdemona

looked.   Her portly form as well as her
comely face seemed, to use a bold figure,
wreathed in smiles.   In fact, she had a com-
munication to make of such uncommon interest that she might be excused for feeling
happy.

She rose, when the time came, and begged
to be allowed to say something.

She had long felt an inward satisfaction,
she said, in marking the rise, progress, and
development of those warmer feelings which
such an atmosphere as that of the Abbey was
certain to generate.   In this case, she had
observed with peculiar gratification that the
interests she was watching advanced with a
smoothness only possible in the calm retirement of a monastery.   Also that there were
no discords, no harsh notes to clash with the
general harmony ; no one was jealous or
envious of another ; each with each, damoi-
seau with damoiselle, was free, unhindered,
to advance his own suit.   "And now," said
Desdemona expansively, "these suits have
all been advanced, they have all prospered"
here there was a general sensation—"and I
am enabled to announce that this Abbey of

Thelema will before long cease to exist because the end proposed by its original Founder has been already attained.

" My friends, Brother Bayard is engaged to Sister Cecilia."

Here there was great cheering.

" Brother Benedict is engaged to Sister Audry."

At each name there was a loud burst of applause.

They were all engaged, every one. And though there was one Sister besides Desdemona for whom there would be no Monk of the Order in consequence of the expulsion of Brother Peregrine and the defection of Paul Rondelet, yet even that loss, which might have caused a discord, was met by an engagement with one of the outer world. There yet remained, however, Miranda.

" And lastly, dear Sisters and friends," said Desdemona, "before I make my final announcement, let us drop a tear together over the Abbey we have loved so well. The highest happiness, as our Founder thought, is to be bound by no rules but those of gentlehood ; to own no obligations but those which spring of culture, good breeding and sweet dispositions; to do what we will for a space within these walls; to be an example to one another of sympathy, thought for others, and good temper. Alas! my friends, the Abbey is no more. We have held our last Function; we must now dissolve.

> "'Brief as the lightning in the collyed night,
> And ere a man hath power to say, Behold!
> The jaws of darkness do devour it up:
> So quick bright things come to conclusion.'

But now for my last announcement. Brother Hamlet, my Brothers and Sisters"—everybody looked at Alan—"is Brother Hamlet no more; that Brother whom we loved, but whose erratic courses we deplored, must have changed his name had the Abbey continued. What name could he have taken but—Brother Ferdinand?"—here Miranda blushed very sweetly. "But he is Alan still, and he has found, O my Sisters, he has found the only woman in the world who is fit to mate with him.

> "'For several virtues
> Have I liked several women: never any
> With so full soul, but some defect in her

> Did quarrel with the noblest grace she owed,
> And put it to the foil : but she—O she !—
> So perfect and so peerless, is created
> Of every creature's best—' "

The actress ceased to act ; she loved all the Sisters, but she loved Miranda most ; her voice broke, and she sat down burying her face in her hands.

It was at eleven o'clock that they all sallied forth to bid Godspeed to bride and bridegroom. They were to ride to the quiet place, fifteen miles away, where they were to spend their honeymoon. Tom lifts his bride into the saddle, springs into his own, and with a storm of cheers and good wishes, they clatter together down the avenue of the Abbey, two black figures against the bright moonlight, and disappear in the dark shadows of the trees.

THE END.

PRINTED BY BILLING AND SONS.

Trieste

Trieste Publishing has a massive catalogue of classic book titles. Our aim is to provide readers with the highest quality reproductions of fiction and non-fiction literature that has stood the test of time. The many thousands of books in our collection have been sourced from libraries and private collections around the world.

The titles that Trieste Publishing has chosen to be part of the collection have been scanned to simulate the original. Our readers see the books the same way that their first readers did decades or a hundred or more years ago. Books from that period are often spoiled by imperfections that did not exist in the original. Imperfections could be in the form of blurred text, photographs, or missing pages. It is highly unlikely that this would occur with one of our books. Our extensive quality control ensures that the readers of Trieste Publishing's books will be delighted with their purchase. Our staff has thoroughly reviewed every page of all the books in the collection, repairing, or if necessary, rejecting titles that are not of the highest quality. This process ensures that the reader of one of Trieste Publishing's titles receives a volume that faithfully reproduces the original, and to the maximum degree possible, gives them the experience of owning the original work.

We pride ourselves on not only creating a pathway to an extensive reservoir of books of the finest quality, but also providing value to every one of our readers. Generally, Trieste books are purchased singly - on demand, however they may also be purchased in bulk. Readers interested in bulk purchases are invited to contact us directly to enquire about our tailored bulk rates. Email: customerservice@triestepublishing.com

You May Also Like

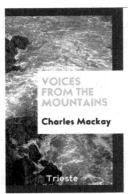

ISBN: 9780649730360
Paperback: 140 pages
Dimensions: 5.25 x 0.30 x 8.0 inches
Language: eng

Voices from the Mountains

Charles Mackay

Report of the Second Annual Meeting of the Maryland State Bar Association, Held at Ocean City, Maryland, July 28-29, 1897

Conway W. Sams

ISBN: 9780649724185
Paperback: 130 pages
Dimensions: 6.14 x 0.28 x 9.21 inches
Language: eng

www.triestepublishing.com

You May Also Like

ISBN: 9780649587667
Paperback: 176 pages
Dimensions: 6.14 x 0.38 x 9.21 inches
Language: eng

Second Year Language Reader

Franklin T. Baker & George R. Carpenter & Katharine B. Owen

ISBN: 9780649692613
Paperback: 120 pages
Dimensions: 6.14 x 0.25 x 9.21 inches
Language: eng

Results of Astronomical Observations Made at the Sydney Observatory, New South Wales, in the Years 1877 and 1878

H. C. Russell

www.triestepublishing.com

You May Also Like

1807-1907 The One Hundredth Anniversary of the incorporation of the Town of Arlington Massachusetts

Various

ISBN: 9780649420544
Paperback: 108 pages
Dimensions: 6.14 x 0.22 x 9.21 inches
Language: eng

Biennial report of the Board of State Harbor Commissioners, for the two fiscal years commencing July 1, 1890, and ending June 30, 1892

Various

ISBN: 9780649194292
Paperback: 44 pages
Dimensions: 6.14 x 0.09 x 9.21 inches
Language: eng

You May Also Like

ISBN: 9780649199693
Paperback: 48 pages
Dimensions: 6.14 x 0.10 x 9.21 inches
Language: eng

Biennial report of the Board of State Harbor Commissioners for the two fisca years. Commeneing July 1, 1884, and Ending June 30, 1886

Various

ISBN: 9780649196395
Paperback: 44 pages
Dimensions: 6.14 x 0.09 x 9.21 inches
Language: eng

Biennial report of the Board of state commissioners, for the two fiscal years, commencing July 1, 1890, and ending June 30, 1892

Various

Find more of our titles on our website. We have a selection of thousands of titles that will interest you. Please visit

www.triestepublishing.com

Lightning Source UK Ltd.
Milton Keynes UK
UKOW06f0953231017
311488UK00005B/1112/P